"This is the beginning of the end of your problems. Right here, right now," Dr. Stevens said. She looked at the ground and drew in a sharp breath, then her eyes were on me, pooling with tears. "You'll have to learn to trust one another."

"Lord of the Flies," Kate said, putting an arm around Connor Bloom, the biggest guy in the group. "You and me to the end."

I knew it wasn't going to be like that; but all the same, allegiances were being made. The weak were already being set aside.

Dr. Stevens opened the van door and got in, staring at us through the open window.

"I can't fix you, but he can. A cure is waiting for each of you down that path."

And then, just like that, she was gone and we were alone.

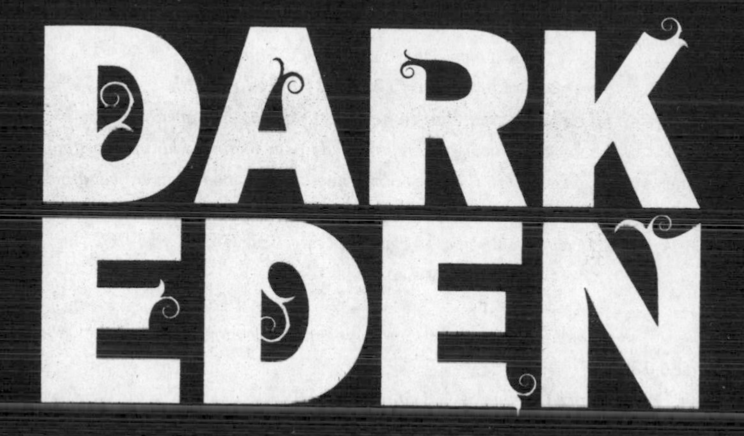

PATRICK CARMAN

Illustrated by
PATRICK ARRASMITH

Katherine Tegen Books is an imprint of HarperCollins Publishers.
Dark Eden

www.epicreads.com

Library of Congress Cataloging-in-Publication Data
Carman, Patrick.
Dark Eden / Patrick Carman. — 1st ed.
p. cm.
Summary: While hiding out in a bomb shelter, Will Besting uncovers shocking secrets about nearby Fort Eden, a mysterious, remote treatment center where Will and six other fifteen-year-olds were sent for radical treatments to cure their phobias.
ISBN 978-0-06-200971-5 *(pbk.)*
[1. Phobias—Fiction. 2. Psychotherapy—Fiction. 3. Interpersonal relations—Fiction.] I. Title.
PZ7.C21694Dap 2011 2011019389
[Fic]—dc23 CIP
AC

Typography by Joel Tippie
12 13 14 15 16 LP/RRDH 10 9 8 7 6 5 4 3 2 1
❖
First paperback edition, 2012

For Cassie and Sierra.
Keep the lights on.

DARK
EDEN

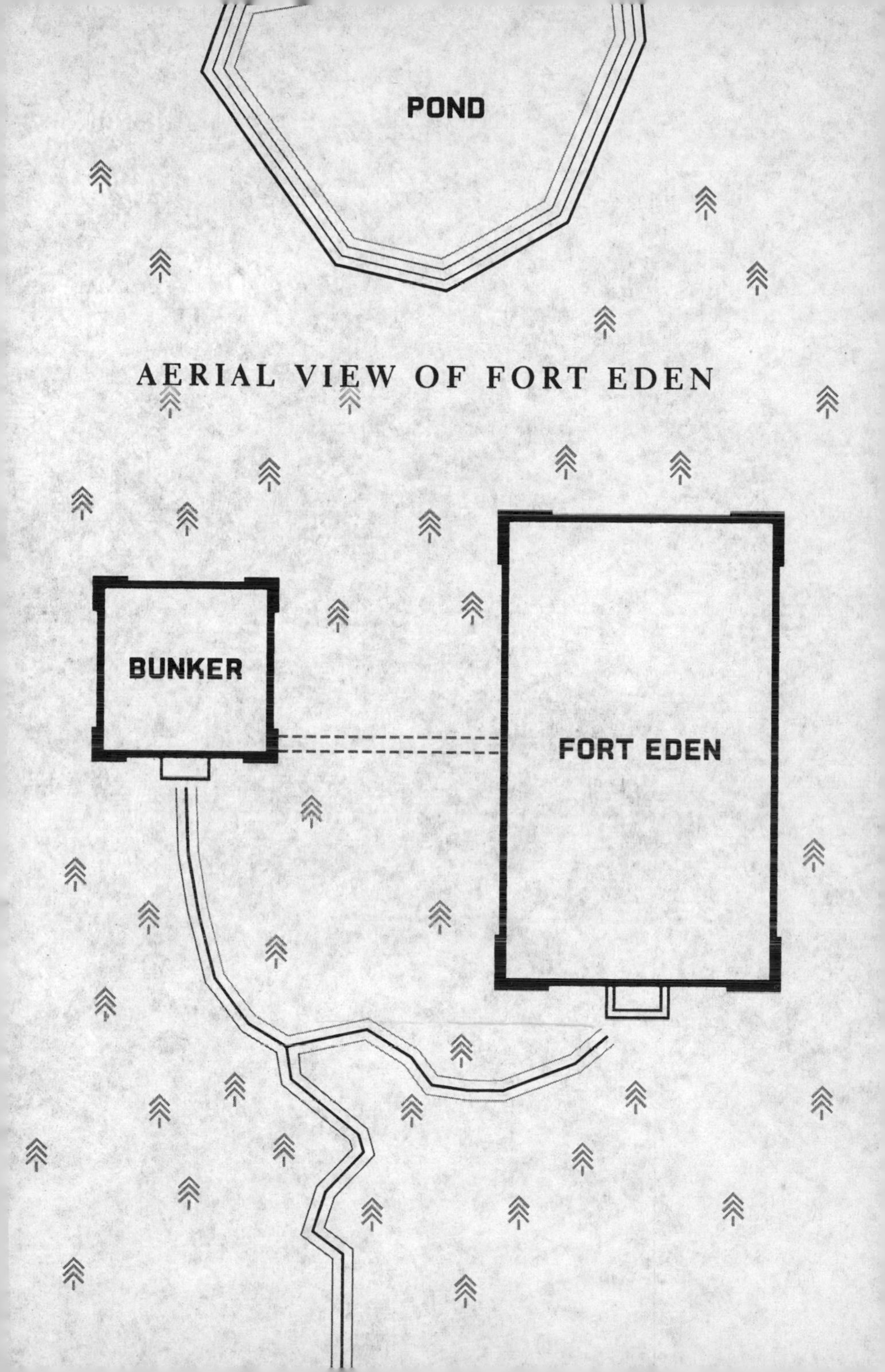
POND
AERIAL VIEW OF FORT EDEN
BUNKER
FORT EDEN

ARRIVAL

Why are you hiding in this room all alone?

There will be no shortage of questions about Fort Eden, the seven, Rainsford, Davis, Mrs. Goring, the *program*. But the first question, the one that will set all things in motion, will be a simple one. It will be asked when they find me.

We asked you a question, Will. Why are you hiding in this room all alone?

I've thought about how I will answer. I won't like

being cornered. I won't like seeing the door blocked by a person I will be forced to speak with. Better I have the answer memorized so they'll let me out into the woods where I can run.

Because I knew.

That's what I'll say when they ask.

I knew, and I was afraid.

WILLIAM BESTING, S167
DR. CYNTHIA STEVENS
6.12.2010

There are more like you. You're not the only one, Will.

How do you mean, more like me?

You're not the only one who's afraid. Lots of people your age are afraid of things. The world can feel scary when you're fifteen. But for some people, like you, certain things are much scarier than they should be. You know this. We've talked about it. But you don't have to be alone; there are others like you.

Why are you telling me this?

I was looking at my notes before you came in today. We've been meeting a long time. Too long, Will.

Wait, what?

Do you trust me, Will? Really trust me?

I guess so. Sure.

Then I'll tell you the truth. I can't help you. I want to, but I can't. And there are others like you, six to be exact. Six others I can't help. Six others who are afraid like you are afraid. And there's a place I want you all to go.

You mean me and six people I've never met? How old are they?

Same age as you.

I'm not doing that. You can't make me.

Your parents want you to go. I've already asked them.

I think they might be growing tired of my lack of progress. One hundred and sixty-seven sessions, Will. Over two years. Don't you see? I can't help you. But I think someone else can.

Where's this place I'm not going to, and who are these people I won't be meeting when I don't get there?

After that the screen on her phone lit up, and she glanced away from me as I watched. Dr. Stevens was a tall, lean woman of about forty. She was blond and pretty and wore smart, rimmed glasses, all of which were a constant distraction. She had a crooked front tooth, which should have marred an otherwise beautiful face, but it was disarming and natural. In my opinion it was the thing that made the whole package, the ribbon.

Excusing herself, she left the room, which was on the third floor of a converted row house that she shared with three other counselors. She left the door a few inches ajar; and I knew when her foot touched the fourth step down, because the stair creaked loudly enough for me to hear from inside the room. Far away, at the bottom of the stairs, I heard the soft sound of a door closing. She'd gone outside onto the front porch to call someone, or so it seemed. The quiet hum of voices drifted in from another room like a cat purring down a dark alley, and I got up from my chair.

We'd been meeting for so long, it was as if Dr. Stevens was my aunt or a much older sister. Sometimes she'd eat lunch while we met; other times she'd take a break and go to the bathroom or to the kitchen downstairs, leaving me to rummage through her things as I waited for the sound of the fourth step on the stairs.

She should have known better than to leave me alone. She shouldn't have scared me like she did. Looking through her things had become a bad habit, like shoplifting a newspaper you weren't even going to read and then finding you were taking something that wasn't yours every time you walked into a store. That's the way it is with secrets. They pile one on top of the other until it's like a house of cards that requires a lot of work to maintain.

It's been a long time since I took my first file from Dr. Stevens's office. If I was building a house of cards, I'd be on my second deck by now. Looking back, there are a few sessions that stick in my memory more completely than all the others.

SESSION NUMBER 12

I thought Dr. Stevens might be reading my future in

the tea leaves at the bottom of her cup, but she was only thirsty for more caffeine, fuel for another half hour with Will Besting. A few keystrokes on her laptop and down the stairs she went, leaving me alone in the room for the first time. I got up from my chair, sat in hers, and looked at the screen of her laptop.

Her computer was locked, but that was easily undone. Dr. Stevens was careless in her keystrokes, a password much too short and too easy for searching eyes like mine. I could only catch her fingers on the first two strokes—*c* and the *a*—then the dart of her skinny index finger up to the keys above. She punched four or five more keys with speed and precision as I pretended to look out the window, my head turned one way and my eyes another.

The password had started with *c-a* and probably continued up there, on that top row, with her long white pointing finger: a *t*.

cat

I won't lie; it was a thrill from the start, sitting in her chair with my fingers flying over the keys, trying to unlock her secrets. Secrets about me. About her.

catplay. catonroof. cathairball. catcatcat. catfood

The fourth step creaked, and I flew back into my own

chair, gripping the wooden arms as Dr. Stevens reentered the room from behind me, her cup filled once more.

A half hour later as we said our farewell, my eye caught a line of books sitting on a shelf. There were four, but only one mattered: the one with a blue background and a cat on the front tipping its striped hat and smiling happily.

catinhat

A password I would come to know all too well.

SESSION NUMBER 19

I found my own folder, filled with audio transcripts. I'd known she was recording all of our sessions—even consented to it—but somehow seeing them there, all stacked up with dates on them, bothered me. It was as if she'd dug deep into my soul and yanked out the secret parts, then stored them like little coffins in a meat locker.

I discovered that my parents had betrayed me, too. For years I'd kept an audio diary of my own that dated all the way back to 2005. I was just a nine-year-old kid when I started, back when I loved to hear my own voice. Dr. Stevens had them all, including the ones where the trouble started.

SESSION NUMBER 31

I kept a chain around my neck after that, from which a silver St. Christopher's medallion hung loosely under my shirt. The medallion was oval shaped—as thick as three sticks of gum—and if I pulled St. Christopher apart at the middle, he was something more useful. St. Christopher's detached lower half was a flash drive, with space enough on it for many, many audio files.

catinhat

I touched the folder marked WILL BESTING, dragged it across the screen, and fed its contents into St. Christopher.

SESSION NUMBER 167

And so it was that whenever Dr. Stevens left the room with her phone in hand, I took something more, something I'd told myself I wouldn't touch.

catinhat

I was in, my heart racing as it always did when I sat in her chair. I'd long since found my way around. I knew where all the patient audio files were. I could have listened to them at my leisure while lying on my bed at home eating jelly beans. But I hadn't done that, not ever. I'd only ever taken my own things, because I'd felt then as I do now that they belonged chiefly to me, not to my parents or to Dr. Stevens.

There had always been a certain folder I'd wanted to explore. It was a folder that enticed me like the smell of buttery popcorn from our kitchen, reaching all the way down the hall and into my room.

THE 7

All the other folders had patient names or dates or benign categories attached to them. But this one—THE 7—what did it mean? She was a doctor, so it had to be seven patients. But why these seven? And why put their information in a folder by themselves, apart from all the others?

What had she said to me? *I can't help you. I want to, but I can't. And there are others like you, six to be exact. Six others I can't help. Six others who are afraid like you are afraid. And there's a place I want you all to go.*

I pulled St. Christopher apart at the middle. The drive free in my hand, I carefully inserted it into the USB port. The saint's silver legs stuck straight out, making it look as if his head was inside Dr. Stevens's computer, looking around for THE 7, peering inside folders as he searched for what was mine.

I didn't look inside just then; I simply dragged the

folder over to the drive and watched as dozens of audio files copied into my possession.

I didn't have to open the folder to know what I would find inside. I'd find my own name there. There were six others, and there was me.

I was one of the seven.

═══

During the months that followed, Dr. Stevens and my parents tried to convince me that a week away from home was going to finally put my problem behind me. No one was calling the opportunity by its true name; instead they used the gentle hook of camp, as in summer camp, with a bunch of my pals riding in canoes and shooting arrows. The arrows and the canoes and the pals, I knew, were not to be. I understood what I was really being asked to do and what they all thought of me. They imagined I was incurable. They were pulling out the stops, going for broke.

"We're looking for a breakthrough," my dad said, his eyes pleading for a yes and the tone in his voice suggesting that I was ten and the two of us were chums. "Dr. Stevens thinks it will work, and we believe her. Just give it a shot."

"Tell Will what she told us," my mom added, touching my dad's hand. "About this Rainsford fellow."

"The only reason you're even going is because the guy trained Dr. Stevens like twenty years ago. He's some sort of genius. There's a program he offers right outside of LA, very exclusive, *very* expensive. And she's getting you in for practically nothing."

"You see? We only want the best for you," my mother added.

"Why can't I go alone?" I asked.

"Because it's a bunch of people working on this stuff together," my dad insisted. "It's not like seeing Dr. Stevens. It's different is all."

"You mean group therapy, like for crazy people."

My dad threw his hands up and walked into the kitchen, but then he turned back and put his palms on the dining-room table where my mom and I sat.

"Just think about it, okay? We think it's the best thing for you."

Weeks went by in which I pleaded with my parents, but there came a moment five days before my departure when I realized they weren't going to let me stay home. I knew this primarily because of my younger brother, Keith, who was startlingly accurate about predicting my parents' intentions.

"You're going; it's already decided," he told me. We were sitting on the floor in my room playing Berzerk on an old Atari 2600 that I'd gotten on eBay. He was wearing the same lime green baseball cap he always wore, pulled down low so his hair spiked up around the sides of his ears. The game, like so many from that era, made some of the most excellent robot sounds I'd ever heard. They were the kinds of sounds that got stuck in my head and danced around until dawn. When the robots found you, they'd chase you around with a monotone warning: *Intruder alert! Intruder alert!* It sounded like an electronic voice speaking into a spinning fan.

My scores were so much higher than his that I felt sorry for him—my Achilles' heel. Never feel sorry for a younger brother in a competitive situation because he'll always get you in the end.

"You're sure?" I asked, not taking my eyes off a 2D robot walking stupidly across the screen.

"They've got that look. It's over."

Keith was thirteen and gangly and popular. He was quiet and mysterious like me, but a much better athlete. One day I'm killing him at air hockey in the garage—a meaningless achievement—and the next thing I know, he's wiping the basketball court with my face, which really mattered.

"Just go," he said, standing up to leave but hanging back to observe a little longer, drinking in the gaming skills he'd later use to obliterate me. "It's not gonna kill you."

When I turned to look at him he was gone, like a ghost who'd delivered a crummy message only to disappear when I needed him the most. Sometimes I felt as if Keith was the older brother, not me. I sat at my desk and stared out the window at the street below as my laptop whirled to life.

For the next three hours I listened to the voices of the seven—including my own—and played Berzerk, my mind melting into a sea of purple robots and bizarre fears I knew nothing about.

What she couldn't have known as we sat next to each other in the backseat of a van heading out of LA was how well I already knew her.

Marisa Sorrento's voice—like everyone else's in the van that day—startled me when I heard it in person for the first time. I'd wondered what it would be like, connecting a voice I knew intimately with a real body and a real face. Marisa Sorrento, the one whose voice I'd liked the best, the one I was most drawn to.

"Can you believe our parents are making us do this?" she asked. Before I could answer, someone else broke in.

"It might be fun, like camp." This voice I also knew. Alex Hersch, whose parents had clearly sold the week to him in the same way it had been sold to me. Knowing what I knew about Alex, coupled with the fact that we were heading into the wilderness, I thought it was a miracle that he hadn't thrown open the van door and hurled himself onto the pavement.

A conversation ensued in the rows ahead of me, and my attention drifted back to Marisa. She was Latina, which I had guessed because of her name; but if it hadn't been for that, I might not have said so. Her voice, like her cinnamon-colored skin, was soft and almost too perfect. While I had been listening to her, I had felt that it was the voice of someone trying very hard to cover any sign of an accent. She lived with her mom and a sister, I knew, and there was some mystery surrounding the death of her dad several years back. Her eyes were dark brown pools that searched mine, waiting for a reply. What had she asked me again?

Can you believe our parents are making us do this?

I shook my head no, I couldn't believe it. But the question had been around too long, and the answer didn't connect. I looked like an idiot.

"Are you feeling okay?" she asked, her eyes crinkling into crow's feet.

"Yeah," I managed. "I'm fine. How are you?"

Oh my God, what a moron. My face was burning up. My tongue felt like sandpaper.

"I don't know," she said, shaking her head just enough that her black ponytail swished back and forth. "Doesn't this whole thing seem a little weird? I don't even know these people."

This was nice, as if she and I were us and everyone else was them. If only my throat wasn't tightening up. I felt as if I was sucking a chocolate milkshake through a swizzle stick.

"You're sure you're okay, right?" she asked again, leaning away from me as if I might throw up on her blue sweatshirt at any moment. And then it happened, the thing I'd feared would happen. My mind seized on a thought: I couldn't be the only one in this van who knew at least something about what was going down.

Was everyone looking at me while I struggled to catch my breath? Everyone in this van was sick, sick with fear or something worse.

What's wrong with Will Besting? Hey, everyone, look at him. No, seriously. Look at him!

I kept telling myself to calm down, I knew better, everything was fine. These people had never met me, and I'd never met them. They'd never even met each other, so they weren't a clique I couldn't be a part of. I knew them better than they knew themselves. I knew their secrets and their fears. I knew they were just as messed up as I was.

If Dr. Stevens or my parents thought for one second I was going anywhere with any of them, they were sorely mistaken.

I'd sooner swim in a pond full of piranhas.

I stared out the window of the van after that, imagining my brother, Keith, in my room going toe-to-toe with robots. I'd be gone a week, and when I returned, the long line of high-score holders that ran down the home screen wouldn't say

WILL

WILL

WILL

and more WILL.

And they wouldn't all say KEITH either, because that's not the way it works. Bloodthirsty younger brothers are smarter than that. All ten slots would be filled, straight down the screen.

GOOD

LUCK

BEATING

ME

NOW

KEITH!

KEITH!

KEITH!

KEITH!

KEITH!

I should have locked my door and crawled out the window so he couldn't touch my stuff.

The van turned off the main highway onto a country road, and Dr. Stevens started talking. She told us we were heading into the mountains now and began reeling off instructions. This had the effect of shutting up everyone as she droned on about how we were all going to get to know each other, how great it was all going to be.

"I want each of you to think about this week as the beginning of the end," she instructed, turning onto a gravel road. "The end of the weight you've carried around for too long. Lean on each other, get to know one another. And let the process take its course."

I was getting my first look at these people after having heard their voices for weeks on end. There was Connor Bloom, a big guy with a crew cut, the kind of athlete that dominated where brute force was a key asset on the field. Alex Hersch's facade didn't fit the stereotypical brainy type—he was more GQ than I'd expected, but I knew better. Alex was smarter than all of us put together. He just preferred we didn't know it. Ben Dugan was both skinny and short, a condition that lowered his confidence where girls were concerned. But I liked him right off because he didn't have that short-guy quality of being in your face all the time. Avery Varone was dark haired and pretty and quiet; Kate Hollander was blond and beautiful and overbearing—both matching pretty much what I'd expected. And Marisa Sorrento was everything I'd hoped for: a sweet smile, perfect skin, nervous but in control. And, importantly, she didn't seem entirely out of my reach. If I had the guts to ask her out, it felt possible that she wouldn't laugh in my face.

We would drive four miles on the gravel road, where I would hear the crunching sound of our wheels crushing rocks. I knew this. I had seen the map taking up space in the folder marked THE 7. After that, two more miles on a dirt road lined with random trails shooting off into the woods. On the map the trails had reminded me of the roots on a huge weed I'd pulled in my own backyard a week before. Four miles down a gravel road, two miles down a weedy-looking dirt road, and farther still. What would I feel if I were these people? I knew how far we had to go and what we'd find when we got there, but no one else did. There was a stillness in the group until we reached a locked gate across the road and Dr. Stevens got out of the van and opened it.

"We're not in Kansas anymore," someone said, and everyone laughed nervously.

It was a girl, Kate Hollander, sitting in the passenger seat next to Dr. Stevens. She was unapproachable for mere mortals, which made what I knew about her seem untrue. If I hadn't heard her say certain things, I'd have categorized them as lies about a popular girl told by her enemies behind her back.

We drove another half mile, descending steeply into a thick forest of trees. The road was a washboard, jarring me so violently that my teeth chattered. I glanced at Marisa, who was staring out the window like everyone else. I wanted to reach out and touch her shoulder and tell her this was all going to be okay, but I knew better. She'd lost interest in me like all the rest. I was a ghost to these people.

The road came to an end, and Dr. Stevens turned the van around, pointing it back up the steep road. The van doors were thrown open and everyone got out, strapping on backpacks bursting with provisions.

"Stay to the right, it's less than a mile," Dr. Stevens said. She was standing before us, one hand still on the door handle as if it was a life preserver.

Ben Dugan, who was a head shorter than I was, turned ashen.

"You're not coming with us?"

I expected the rest of the group to laugh. Under different circumstances I'm sure they would have; but they were just as attached to Dr. Stevens as Ben was, and we were standing in the middle of nowhere. None of us wanted to forge the path alone.

"This is the beginning of the end of your problems.

Right here, right now," Dr. Stevens said. She looked at the ground and drew in a sharp breath, then her eyes were on me, pooling with tears. "You'll have to learn to trust one another."

"Lord of the Flies," Kate said, putting an arm around Connor Bloom, the biggest guy in the group. "You and me to the end."

I knew it wasn't going to be like that; but all the same, allegiances were being made. The weak were already being set aside.

Dr. Stevens opened the van door and got in, staring at us through the open window.

"I can't fix you, but he can. A cure is waiting for each of you down that path."

And then, just like that, she was gone and we were alone.

"No signal, that's just great."

Ben Dugan was holding his cell phone over his head, squinting into the sun, hoping for a lifeline out of the wilderness.

"Anyone *not* on Sprint?" Connor asked, scratching

his short-cropped hair with the back of his knuckles and waving his phone around, trying to lure in a signal (or maybe a lightning bolt, it was hard to tell).

"We haven't had any service for an hour," said Marisa. "Where have you guys *been*?"

No patience for dumb boys, I thought. *Noted.*

Everyone had switched to taking pictures in the absence of text messages flying back and forth about a wild adventure they were on. Better to at least have something to post online when it was all over than to arrive on Facebook with nothing to show for a week off the grid. Doing nothing was out of the question. They had to be doing *something*, better still if it was terribly interesting.

As we walked, I looked overhead from my position at the back of the line in search of the sun but couldn't find it. Tall trees full of green needles crowded the sky. We wound back and forth through deep forest, and a pair of crows cawed angrily, following us at a distance.

The path was wide enough for two people to walk side by side, and when we'd begun, it was Kate and Connor at the front. Ben Dugan had fallen into step with Alex Hersch, the two of them already acting as if they'd known each other a long time. Marisa walked beside the quietest of us all, the one I'd been most curious about, the one named Avery. She'd been in a bunch of foster homes during the past few years, and wasn't doing so well in the one she was in when we departed, either. Marisa drifted back and fell into step at my side as I took a deep breath, the smell of pine and dirt kicked up on the path filling my lungs.

"Wow, she's quiet," Marisa whispered in my direction. "Kind of like you."

I imagined me and Avery in a room, the blistering two-word conversation that would occur.

Hi, she would say.

Hi, I would say back.

A morbid silence would settle in, and we'd stare at our shoes.

Afternoon had arrived, and a late September heat was building as Marisa peeled off her sweatshirt.

"It's the same for you, right?" Marisa said, the two of us falling behind the group seven or eight steps. "You've never met any of them?"

I glanced at her red T-shirt and tried to read the words written in black letters across her chest but failed. The angle was all wrong.

"I don't know them," I said. Strictly speaking, this was

a lie, but what else was I going to say? *Actually, I know everything there is to know about all of these people, including you.*

I tried once more to read the words on her shirt, and my eyes fell on her bare arm, which didn't look very different from a deep California tan I'd seen a thousand times before.

"Alex is cute," she said. "Too bad he's gay."

"Really?" I said, the word out of my mouth so quickly I couldn't take it back. I was having a conversation with her, or something like one.

"Sure he is. He spent four or five hours shopping at REI, loading up for this thing. Nobody looks that good unless they really work at it."

I didn't exactly see how this added up to anything more than preparedness, or maybe some kind of OCD, but what did I know?

"Where do you go to school?" she asked me. "What grade are you in? Let me guess: junior, private school, very exclusive."

Wrong on all three counts, but I nodded yes. The truth? Homeschooled, technically a junior, but I'd been fast about my business so I was already doing freshman college courses online. The exclusive part, on second thought, was truer than she knew. I was a school of one.

I made a last attempt to glimpse the words on her shirt, and this time she noticed.

"Whatever," she said; and just like that, she was taking two steps to my one, the distance between us growing by the second.

Was it my persistent glances at her curvy chest that bothered her, or was it my wordless nod of yes to her questions? Either way, I'd blown it.

"Wait," I said before she caught up to the rest. She turned, back-peddling away, and I finally saw the words on her shirt.

I WANNA BE ADORED.

That can be arranged, I thought. A good line if only I could have said it out loud, or possibly a really bad one she'd heard a hundred times already. I knew there was more to the message on the shirt then met the eye, and I wanted to say so; but my mouth turned as dry as dust on the path as she stopped and waited for me to catch up. I walked toward her, and it felt as if the world was tilting in my favor, if only for a split second.

"What is it, Will? What do you want?"

I wanted to say, *My dad drives a delivery truck, my mom does alterations, I like your shirt, I don't go to school.*

But I didn't. The closer I got, the more nervous I felt. My mind drew a blank, and I stared off into the trees.

Marisa shook her head and started up the path until she caught up with Avery, after which the two of them walked in silence. I hooked my thumbs behind the straps of my backpack and followed.

Everyone arrived at the fork in the trail, gathering like a flock of ducklings behind Kate and Connor.

"Come on, hurry up," Ben yelled back at me, and the pack of six moved on toward the right. I coasted farther back because I knew we were getting close. Pretty soon the path would end and I'd miss my chance. Marisa offered one more fleeting look over her shoulder, our eyes meeting, and then she was gone.

They were all of them gone, and I was alone at the fork, listening as their voices mingled with the wind in the trees and grew softer.

After a time, I couldn't hear them at all.

The path to the left could hardly be called a trail at all. Everything in the wild of the forest seemed to cave in on itself the deeper I went, leaving little more than a bead of dirt running a line through thick underbrush. The trees remained, swaying ominously over my head; and there were crows, more of them now, watching my every move like sentries on a castle wall. I sensed a clearing to my right and left the trail altogether, hoping to catch a glimpse of the other six.

Crawling along the floor of the woods was easy enough, like making a tunnel in a cornfield, and before I knew it I'd come to the very edge. I didn't dare poke my head out of the thicket; I didn't need to. I could see what lay before me through the crush of undergrowth just fine: a hidden place, rising unexpectedly out of the dirt. I knew what it was. I had the map from the folder marked THE 7.

Fort Eden.

The place sent a chill of dread down my spine from the moment I saw it. Low slung to the ground, made entirely of concrete slabs crawling with moss and vines. My first impression was of a massive casket left alone in the woods for years and years, overrun by a menacing forest of gloom. At the same time, I couldn't help thinking of the old Eden, the one in the Bible. Eden was supposed to be this perfect place where nothing ever died and people were always happy. But the fort was like the anti-Eden, the place left over after the fall of mankind. The woods were still woods, but they were wild and tangled and dark. There were no perfect days here, no laughing people.

I saw them all—the six—standing in front of the fort with worried looks on their faces. Even confident Kate Hollander was rattled.

"This can't be right," she said, her voice floating through the clearing in crystal-clear shards.

"We could go back," Ben said, which is when everyone seemed to notice all at once that I wasn't there. Words pinged sharply against my ears, as if they were fired from the barrel of a pellet gun.

Alex: *Whoa. Spooky. What was his name again?*

Connor: *Will! Hey, come out, man.*

Ben: *Should we go back and look for him?*

Kate: *I'm just saying, if they think we're living in that thing for a week, they can forget it.*

Marisa: *Seriously, Kate?*

Avery: *(Sullen, voiceless).*

I glanced from side to side, taking in the whole of the clearing, sizing up my options. There was the fort, a rectangle slab of hard corners with one giant door at the front and barred windows along its sides. A hundred feet to the left sat a smaller building, just as ghoulishly unappealing as Fort Eden. From the map I knew this was the Bunker, whatever that meant. A huge, fallen tree lay against its corner where the trunk had snapped in two, the top half resting like a dead animal on the flat roof. The pinecones and needles of the tree were long since gone, replaced by a swarm of brown mushrooms and clumps of stringy green moss. On the other side of Fort Eden, a pathway led into the woods, beyond which I knew there was a pond.

Before the others could make up their minds about whether they should go looking for me or climb the front steps and knock on the door to a lifeless concrete fort, a person came out of the smaller building. I saw her first, because I'd been looking at the Bunker already. She was old, dressed as a person of the woods: a dark flannel shirt, work pants, boots. The woman walked morosely down the cobblestone path, slow and steady.

"Who feels like running?" asked Ben (too loudly, I thought). But then, he would be feeling the terror start to rise at the back of his throat. The deeper we'd gone on the path, the quieter he'd become. He was beginning to sense the presence of things he wanted no part of.

At the midway point of her journey between the

Bunker and Fort Eden, the woman stopped. She was standing directly across from where I hid in the underbrush and was smelling the air like a dog catching a scent. Her gaze settled in my direction, and I had an uneasy feeling in my bones.

She sees me.

Later I would conclude that it had been a trick of the light through the trees. But at the time, hidden as I was and frozen in place, I was convinced that she'd searched the whole of the forest and settled her cobalt eyes directly on my face. Whoever she was, she had a severe face, emotionless and cold. Her hair was nearly white, with small flecks of black around the crown of her head. She grew tired of staring off into the trees, and soon she was stomping up the concrete steps of the fort.

She seemed to take almost no notice of the bewildered group of teenagers until she'd cleared the last stair and turned on them.

"I'm Mrs. Goring, the cook," she said sternly. Her voice was papery but strong. "Not your maid or your mother. Act like grown-ups and I won't spit in your oatmeal."

I got the feeling she was taking this opportunity to make her feelings known before the owner of the place could warn her to leave the guests alone. She hooked her thumbs into the pocket of her jeans. "I'm also the entire maintenance crew: plumber, fix-it woman—the works. If you see something in here you think might break, don't touch it."

Alex Hersch raised his hand.

"I don't remember saying I was a tour guide," Mrs. Goring said. "But I'll take one question. Fire when ready."

"One of us is missing."

Mrs. Goring appeared to be counting heads, as if Alex was either playing games or was just plain stupid.

"So I see," she offered at length. "Where'd they go?"

Alex opened his mouth, but not fast enough to overcome Connor Bloom's team captain persona.

"We think he might have tried to go back home," said Connor, which was news to me.

"Speak for yourself," said Marisa.

Mrs. Goring waved off the entire thing as if it wasn't her problem and, with significant effort, pushed open the door.

"Remember what I said," she concluded. "I'm not a maid. And don't touch things you don't need to."

For some unimaginable reason, Kate walked up the stairs and past Mrs. Goring. This seemed to spur an exodus from the grounds as Connor followed, then Ben and Alex. Avery shrugged and climbed the concrete steps. Marisa gave me one last try, turning to the path and raising her voice to the trees.

"We're going in, Will. If you're out there, we want you to come with us."

I wanted to yell back, *You could come out here with me instead. You don't have to go inside.*

But I couldn't do it. They'd all come running. They'd make me go with them, which was something that just couldn't happen.

Marisa walked up the stairs, and Connor pushed the door closed behind her.

Looking at the empty clearing, I realized my condition with alarming finality.

I was all alone.

Two hours passed in which I didn't move at all other than to scan the buildings and open my backpack. During that time, the wind blew in layers of gray clouds and a soft rain began to fall. I'd come prepared with a hoodie, which I pulled out and put on. I had three dozen Clif Bars and six bottles of water in the backpack, too. That plus a Swiss Army knife, some earbuds, seven pairs of underwear, two white T-shirts, a couple of pairs of socks, my toothbrush, and a bar of soap still in its wrapper. Also, a penlight in my pocket and a rolled-up blanket tied to the outside of my pack. And finally, my Recorder,[1] something I hadn't dared to pull out of my backpack while everyone else was around.

Some people won't go anywhere without a cell phone or a book. I'm like that with my Recorder. I capture

---

[1] History of the Recorder

The first person who saw my Recorder was my brother, Keith. He was eleven; I was thirteen. He'd been stopping in my room every day for weeks, begging for castoffs.

"You don't even need this one. You've got a bunch more just like it."

Once Keith got his weekly allowance, he couldn't wait five minutes before riding his bike to Starbucks for a five-dollar buzz. I was the opposite, a saver; and for the longest time I had no idea what I was even saving *for*.

"Come on, let me borrow ten bucks. I'll totally pay you back."

I might have said yes if Keith hadn't already proven himself a lousy borrower. He's got at least two bankruptcies in his future; and besides, I'd finally figured out what to do with my money.

When I'd turned twelve, my mom introduced me to online college classes at a tech school in India. Shockingly cheap courses taught by thickly accented Indian tech gods about stuff I actually had some interest in. First I took video game programming, then a series on electronics, then hardware integration. I failed approximately half of the classes I took, but my interest was sparked.

I was an audio geek at heart, but I liked video, too. Homebrew degrees in electronics and programming pushed me over the edge. I ended up on craigslist buying up old iPods and digital cameras until my money ran out.

Then I opened them up and started digging around.

"What the hell is that thing?"

Keith was back, guzzling his allowance through a plastic straw, looking over my shoulder.

"It's my Recorder."

"Looks like a seven-hundred-dollar piece of garbage."

"Thanks, Keith. Next time I want your opinion, I'll beat it out of you."

"Oh, really? You and what geek army?"

God, he bugged me bad sometimes. But I could tell he was jealous. Sure my Recorder was basically the same thing as a new iPhone without the phone part; but I'd built it myself, and it looked gnarly.

voices and sounds, sometimes videos, and turn them into something interesting. And I like listening, which is probably what drew me to Dr. Stevens's files in the first place.

Having nothing else to record but my own voice—something I'd heard way too much of lately—I plugged the mic into the Recorder and pointed it into the grove, recording the sounds of nature as shadows crept over Fort Eden.

At 7:00 PM, Mrs. Goring came out of the Bunker and sat heavily on a concrete bench, leaving the door open behind her. I hadn't seen her return from the fort, but maybe there were other doors and other cobblestone paths that wound through the clearing I knew nothing about. She blew her nose ferociously into a rag, then leaned her head back against the hard surface of the Bunker. If not for her occasional movement, I would have guessed she'd fallen asleep.

At 7:10 PM she rose and walked to the back of the Bunker, where I heard the sharp sound of an ax hitting wood.

She's no slouch, Mrs. Goring, I thought. *She can really swing that thing.*

I took the sound as a bad sign. If push came to shove and I had to fight my way out of the compound, I'd rather my enemy was good at Monopoly, not chopping things up.

It was the time of year when night turned colder in the suburbs, but I hadn't counted on how much colder it would be in the mountains at night. I tightened my hoodie down over my ears, a shiver ran through my body, and I wondered what I should do.

No one had come looking for me as I'd expected they might. No search party, not even a friendly plea to come in out of the cold. Maybe they'd already forgotten I existed or never cared to begin with. Or maybe they were all dead. It was possible.

A brown spider twirled a web over my head between the branches, and I watched it anxiously, listening to the sound of Mrs. Goring splitting wood. It occurred to me then that Mrs. Goring was behind the Bunker, where I couldn't see her, which meant she couldn't see me. The Bunker was empty, and the door stood open. I could take my chances and stay outside all night, but how cold and wet would it be at 2:00 AM, and who or what might come searching for me in the darkest part of night? Fort Eden was out of the question. I wouldn't go in there. They couldn't make me.

A deep silence fell over the clearing, and I put my

recording things away. Darkness was coming, and I stood in the gathering gloom, catching my hair in the cobweb overhead and slapping it free as the distant sound of chopping returned.

I took two bottomless breaths, clearing my head as I stared at the door to the Bunker.

And then I ran.

THE DAYS OF OUR CAPTIVITY

BEN

The hulking mass of Fort Eden is alive.

It's about to leap out of the ground like a crouching monster and rip me apart.

Don't look back. Keep running for the door.

What I felt as I ran across the clearing couldn't have been true. It was a nightmarish figment of my imagination, nothing more. But that didn't make it any less disturbing as I stood with my back against the wall inside the Bunker.

I'd made it, but I couldn't stop thinking that Fort Eden itself had been watching me, trying to decide what to do about me.

There you are, Will Besting. I see you running. Intruder alert! Intruder alert!

I shook my head and listened for any sounds that might tell me what to do, taking my Recorder in hand and pointing it around the room. Were there others living in the Bunker who hadn't shown their faces yet? Maybe Mrs. Goring had an insane stepdaughter wearing a white prom dress and clutching a metal yardstick or a baseball bat. If that was true, I'd hear her talking to herself or rapping the weapon against the footboard on her bed. I heard neither sound. For a moment I thought I heard a sniffing, as if from a large and unfriendly animal, but then I realized it was my own nose running down my half-frozen face.

So that was it then; the Bunker would be a quiet place of slab walls and sparse furnishings. Not even a ticking clock. The silence was already gnawing at my insides. It was also chilly inside the Bunker, which was probably why Mrs. Goring had been chopping wood outside as I ran through the clearing.

I walked down a narrow hall, dark and uninviting,

listening for Mrs. Goring's return. I expected to hear my own footsteps creaking on the floor, but the whole place was made of poured concrete, including the floor I stood on. There was something about the dead silence of my movement that scared me. If I could move this quietly, so could someone else. What if there *was* a crazy person living in the Bunker? I wouldn't hear a yardstick swinging for the back of my head until it was too late.

It was smaller inside than I'd expected, which made me think the Bunker walls were two, maybe three feet thick. To the left was a sitting room with two ragged chairs and a kerosene lantern like the one my dad bought at a garage sale many summers ago, thinking we'd use it on a camping trip. The trip had been canceled because Keith had basketball camp, and now the lamp sits in our garage collecting cobwebs.

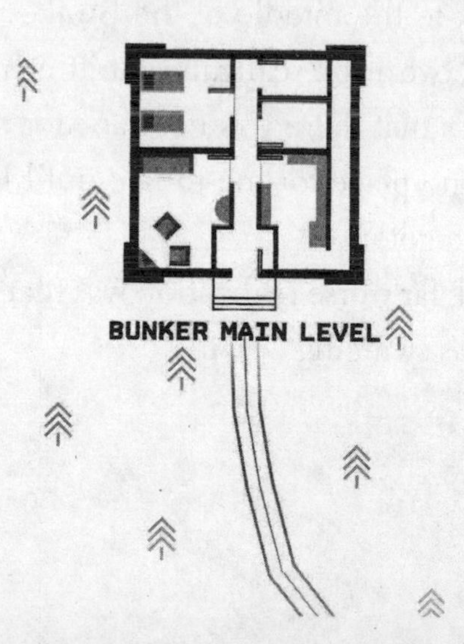

Did the Bunker lack electricity? If so, how did Mrs. Goring cook the food Marisa and the others were going to eat?

In the corner of the room there was a wide, soot-encrusted mouth and black streaks running up the wall: the fireplace.

I kept moving, glancing into the bedroom, where two twin beds sat next to each other in the dark like a pair of rotting teeth. Across from the bedroom, a bathroom I didn't care to explore. I stood at the center point of the Bunker and faced the far end of the hall from which I'd come. It was dark down there, and I could barely see the door where light crept in from the corners. I turned toward the rest of the Bunker, an exact mirror of the first side. Two rooms—a kitchen and a laundry room—with old but very real appliances. So there was electricity.

I went back to the middle of the Bunker and stared down the hall, two awful realizations hitting me at once.

The first was that there was no place for me to hide, and certainly no place for me to live until Dr. Stevens came back and got us.

The second, far worse realization was that the door to the Bunker was swinging open.

I headed for the kitchen because it was the room I hoped she'd come to last. Mrs. Goring would make a fire in the sitting room, maybe kick off her boots and relax there awhile. I crept across the slick floor, careful not to bump into anything that might clang or fall, and arrived in the bleakest part of the room. I crouched down beside a stone counter and, leaning back, discovered that this was no corner but something else: a floor-to ceiling opening three or more feet wide hidden in the darkness.

My hands touched the cold wall behind me just as Mrs. Goring practically floated into the kitchen. She was like a ghostly apparition—so quiet—and I realized she was in her stocking feet. I'd been right about the boots coming off. I crawled in the dark as a lantern was lit in the kitchen, sending dancing shadows down a sloping corridor in front of me.

I was on the other side of the kitchen wall, at the top of a ramp that led down into blackness, which meant that the Bunker had a basement. It had been part of a fort at one time, so it shouldn't have surprised me, but it did.

"Can't wait to cook for these idiots," Mrs. Goring yelled, all the softness gone out of her voice. She was talking to the walls, complaining. On the steps in front of Fort Eden her voice had seemed softer, almost delicate in its authority. But here, in the Bunker, she could really wail.

A thought crossed my mind as Mrs. Goring left the kitchen to check on the fire. I was down a gravel road, a dirt road, a washboard road. I was down a path, into the woods, and into an ancient bunker in the middle of nowhere. But the basement was something worse. It felt eternal and endless and bleak. The rabbit hole that had started in a van in broad daylight had led to an entrance that would take me underground where no one could hear me scream.

I took the penlight out of my front pocket and tapped it on, washing the way down in a slim bead of blue light. It was indeed a ramp, like a narrow sloping driveway, and at the bottom, an open door.

My options were severely limited: descend the ramp or enter the Bunker and deal with Mrs. Goring.

"One step at a time," I told myself, and it would have gone that way for many minutes if Mrs. Goring had not returned to the kitchen. Her nearness bothered me, a lucky thing, because no sooner was I down the ramp and through the open door below than I heard her following behind.

By the time Mrs. Goring started down the ramp I was already underground, making my way along a line of shelves in search of a place to hide. As I clicked off the penlight and the room went harrowingly black, a dizzy spell hit me square in the forehead without warning. I reached out my hand and took hold of a shelf, careful not to knock anything over, and started moving for the back wall.

A light turned on overhead, fluorescent and buzzing, the room awash in pale yellow. There were three rows of shelves, and the two I sat between were filled with food. Boxes of cake mix, bags of flour, cans of tomatoes and soup and . . .

"Hot chocolate, that's what I need. Take off the chill," Mrs. Goring said.

She was at the shelf to my right, sifting through the cans, mumbling to herself. If she'd have been looking for a kid sitting on the floor in the basement, she'd have seen me for sure. But I stayed stone still as she found the container of Nestlé and made for the ramp, shutting off the light as she went.

And she did something else I'd hoped she wouldn't

do—a small thing, really, but meaningful given my circumstances.

She pulled the basement door shut, and from what I could tell, she locked it from the outside.

I was trapped.

The air hockey table at our house is in the basement, where long thin windows run along the edge of the low ceiling so daylight can pour in. My mom constantly set stacks of laundry on the table in order to drive us insane; and sometimes when Keith lost five or six games in a row, he'd randomly change the rules, a sort of air hockey madness taking over the game.

Hand stand!

Face burner!

Elbow shots!

Describing these random Keith rules isn't really necessary. They speak for themselves: pure desperation at a time in our lives when I exterminated him relentlessly. In hindsight I think I did him a favor, toughening him up before the real competition of school and organized sports kicked in. I could have used that kind of training myself, come to think of it.

I was thinking of Keith and how we'd battled in the basement as I sat in the darkness of the Goring bunker. Were there any windows along the top edge, as there were in my own basement back home? It was an important question, because there were risks if I turned on the overhead light. Mrs. Goring might be sitting on the stoop, scaring off the coyotes. What would she do if light washed over the clearing unexpectedly? She would know someone was in the basement. And then there was Fort Eden. I'd seen its barred windows. Everyone inside would see the light. They might think it was Mrs. Goring; they might not.

Listening carefully was useful, because it more or less answered my question and then some. The basement of the Bunker was deathly quiet. I didn't hear the fire crackling upstairs or the sound of Mrs. Goring as she walked back and forth between the rooms. There was no washing machine, no tea pot screaming with the steam of hot water. I couldn't hear the soft wind in the trees or the crows outside.

This was both good and bad news as I got up from the floor and tapped my penlight on. Good, because I could knock over shelves of food down here and no one would hear me. Bad, because no one would hear me if I yelled for help. I double-checked, pointing the light along the ridge of the ceiling to the small room and finding only a gray concrete ridge but no windows. I went to the door that led to the ramp and found the light switch.

I stood in the corner of the basement and checked the door, locked from the outside as I'd feared. My gaze turned to the right—three rows of carefully organized floor-to-ceiling shelves filled with large cans of food and boxes. To my left, a long concrete wall with another door at the far end, which I approached but chose not to open. Better to get the lay of the land first, then I could circle back. I found more shelves against a wall, food and building supplies: scrap wood, jars of nails and rivets, a musty tarp.

I walked to the back of the basement, along the edge of the shelves that held the cans of food, and found one more door. This door was not like the others, which were all made of heavy timber and had iron hinges. The door I stood in front of was made of metal, like a freezer, and on the front a word was stenciled with red paint.

BOMB SHELTER

I don't fear enclosed spaces; in fact, I like them quite a bit more than wide-open cafeterias or ball fields. But the words had the ring of finality. It was a place people went if the world was coming to an end.

There was a pin on a chain holding a freezer handle in place. The pin emitted a sharp sound of metal as I removed it and let it hang from the chain like a body swinging from a noose. The handle was cold in my hand, but it pulled easily enough, and the door to the bomb shelter was open.

A curb ran along the bottom edge, and I stepped over it, peering into a strange and secret place. Before I knew it I was inside, discovering a knob that clicked once and then turned, bringing up the light.

I had come to the farthest corner of where I could go; and, turning around, I pulled the door in close behind me, just shy of locking myself in.

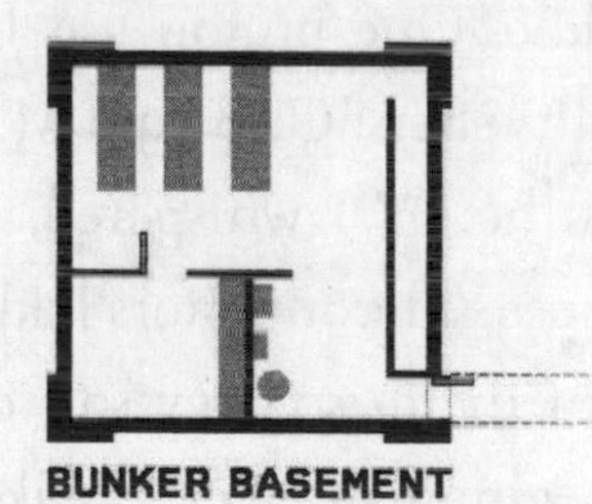

There were many things in the bomb shelter: a drooping cot, a vent trickling earthy air, a toilet in one corner.

There was a fifties-style red phone that emitted no dial tone, shelves with a lot of junk and some yellowed paperbacks, and a power outlet that worked, with a hot plate plugged into it.

But none of these things caught my eye when I'd turned the dimmer switch knob and the light went on. It was the wall of monitors that captured every ounce of my attention.

"No way," I muttered, touching the curved glass of an empty screen. It was a foot across, with a metal housing that was rusting in one corner. And it was not the only screen; there were six more.

There were seven monitors—one in the middle and six wrapped around the outside in a circle, all of them staring vacantly in my direction—and a set of four buttons in the middle. One button was black; the others were marked with letters: *G*, *B*, and *M*.

"Why are you here?" I whispered, staring at a wall that made no sense. The monitors had that old, 1950s-era quality about them, so they sort of fit—but how? The room was beginning to feel less like a bomb shelter and more like a safe room. A room that would allow someone to see outside after the door had been sealed shut from a dangerous world outside. There was a part of me—the same part that had been listening to recordings for weeks—that liked the idea of secretly observing the world outside. This could be interesting.

I set my backpack on the smooth floor, retrieving one of the water bottles and gulping down half of its contents. My finger hovered over the M button, then I pushed it in and a loud, flat click echoed in the bomb shelter. The center monitor sparked to life. It was dim at first, like a retrograde TV that hadn't been used in a long time and needed a few seconds to wake up. As the image grew brighter, I saw them: a group in an open room, sitting around a large table as if they were taking turns telling ghost stories. The light was faint, but I knew these people.

Ben Dugan's back, a mop of dark hair spilling over the neck of a polo shirt. To his right, the shape of Connor Bloom's cropped, domed head. On Ben's left, Alex Hersch. And the faces of the girls as the circle went around: Kate, Avery, Marisa.

I could see that they were talking, but what they were saying was a mystery to me. The monitor was showing, but it wasn't telling. There was no audio whatsoever, and after examining the wall, I found no sign of a speaker or volume control. I felt as if I was ten feet underwater, staring through the filmy surface of a pond at talking heads I couldn't hear. It also felt like a trick or a punishment for what I'd done: the missing half of what I'd stolen. I'd been listening to their disembodied voices for weeks. Now I was seeing them but couldn't hear what they were saying.

The oppressive silence of the bomb shelter made the images feel haunted, as if they were people long since dead and I was watching silent home movies from a hundred years before. Either that or I'd gone totally deaf in the basement of Mrs. Goring's bunker. I squeezed the water bottle in my hand and heard the cheap plastic crinkling between my fingers. At least I hadn't lapsed into a nightmare.

I thought my luck might improve with one of the other buttons, so I pushed in the white G button. When I did, the M button popped back out, and the screen began to fill with the image of a different room. The tube inside the monitor struggled to life, the image fluttering and weak. It was dimmer than the first, and the picture never settled down entirely. Whatever camera it was attached to was pointed directly at a chair, which was empty. Behind the chair was a gray concrete wall with the numbers 2, 5, and 7 stenciled in red, just like the bomb shelter door. I backed away from the monitor, sensing that there was a connection here. Whoever had painted the bomb shelter door had also painted the *2*, the *5*, and the *7*. I suspected that the room was upstairs in the Bunker, and I just hadn't seen it. Either that or it was in Fort Eden.

I crept forward and pushed in the B button. The screen died again, then slowly shimmered back to life. It was the same as the last scene: an empty chair, a gray wall, and four other numbers, stenciled in red: *1*, *3*, *4*, *6*.

"Creepy," I whispered, drinking down the last of the water and hoping that the toilet would flush quietly when the time came to use it. I felt suddenly tired and looked at my watch for the first time in hours: 10:35 PM. How had it gotten so late, so fast?

I sat on the sagging cot to think, staring at the empty room and the four numbers.

"It's us," I said, leaning back on my elbows, feeling the weight of sleep edging closer. "Seven numbers, seven patients. *G* for girls, *B* for boys, *M* for main room."

I was certain of this in the same way that I knew I could return any face burner Keith fired across our air hockey table back home. These numbers were us. These rooms meant something.

I put my arms behind my head and lay back, a heavy feeling on my eyelids.

So quiet. So very, very quiet, like a silent torture chamber that was sucking my will to live.

Keith's voice appeared at the last edge of wakefulness.

Change the channel, Will. This show is ultralame.

And then I was asleep.

The slick floor of the hallway is cold on my body, but I'm so weak I can't get up. The hall is white and long. I am alone, then there's a shadow, far away and moving toward me: a rolling gurney with a body on top, the sound of its wheels rattling. It's close now, the white sheet stained with blood. I want to get up as the cart moves past, but I can't.

Will?

It's Marisa on the gurney, smiling vacantly.

I wanna be adored.

Get up, Will. Get up.

Intruder alert! Intruder alert!

I was off the cot and on my feet, my mind caught between alertness and sleep. Where was I? *The van, the path, Fort Eden, the Bunker, the basement.*

I was lying on a cot in a bomb shelter, not sitting on a white floor watching Marisa roll by. And yet, in the deep silence of the basement, the wheels of the gurney were there. One of the wheels was flapping back and forth as if it was attached to a bad grocery cart.

There was no time to hide and no point in turning off the light in the bomb shelter. Whoever had come into the basement had turned on the main lights, so turning off mine wasn't going to make any difference. I saw shadows roll by through the crack I'd left in the door. The gurney was not only real, it was moving through the basement.

It stopped where they kept the dry goods. I remembered the closed door I'd seen there, the one I hadn't gone back to and opened.

That must be where they keep the bodies.

This thought circled through my brain until the sound of the wheels faded and then almost disappeared entirely.

I looked at my watch: 10:58 PM. I'd only slept for about twenty minutes. Opening the heavy bomb shelter door another inch, I peered into the lit basement and found it empty. From my vantage point I could see that the door leading back upstairs had been left wide-open. I could escape into the woods, or at least into the kitchen. But who would I meet there: Mrs. Goring, standing in the Bunker with a meat cleaver?

I talked myself off the madhouse ledge I'd crawled onto and stepped out into the basement. Whoever had been down here was gone now, through the door I hadn't bothered to open. I went quickly for the ramp that led upstairs, peeking around the corner. No one up there, or so it seemed, but I'd left my backpack in the bomb shelter. I turned to go back and saw light coming from under the door of the room where the gurney had gone. And something more than that—I heard voices. A small cheer, in fact, or something like one, far off down a hallway I couldn't see.

I crept to the door and looked around its edge, hopelessly confused.

"Hands off the cart!"

It was Mrs. Goring's voice, at the top of a much longer ramp. A tunnel, slanting up like the one from the basement to the Bunker, stretched thirty yards or more between two buildings. She was in Fort Eden. And it wasn't a hospital gurney she was pushing but a food cart filled with late-night snacks.

"That's it for tonight. Make the most of it." Mrs. Goring's mouselike voice glided down the tunnel. A door at the far end was slammed shut, and the cart was rolling toward me once more. She passed under the first of five grimy lightbulbs, one every twenty feet, and I backed away from the door.

Stepping quietly toward my hiding place, it occurred to me that I might be able to get across on my own. Maybe if I waited until everyone was asleep I could find out what was really going on without anyone knowing.

Mrs. Goring's empty cart was clamoring down the runway as I reentered the bomb shelter and dialed down the light. Darkness would have engulfed me if not for the glow of the monitor, which I had neglected to turn off. I went to push the black OFF button, just to be extra careful, and that's when I saw it on the screen.

Ben Dugan was sitting in the chair.

I tried to read Ben's lips, but it was no use. Whatever he was saying didn't register on my end. There were pauses, as if he was trying to decide if he should keep going or not. I couldn't stand the silence anymore and took out my Recorder, dialed in BEN DUGAN, and hit PLAY. The funny thing was, watching his face on the screen and hearing his voice in my head almost felt real, like the two belonged together. The first voice in my head was Dr. Stevens's.

When was the first time you felt this way? Go back as far as you can remember.

I don't know. I forget.

What did you forget?

That's an unanswerable question. I don't remember what I forgot.

Right, but there's a clue here, you see? There are things you don't want to remember, so you don't. When you think of these things—the events you don't want recorded in your memory—what are they? What is it about them that make you afraid?

I don't like sand.

Okay. That's a start. So, if you're digging around in the sand, that bothers you?

I wouldn't know. I don't think I've ever done that.

Oh, but you have, Ben. Trust me, you have done this. And you're still alive.

I don't remember.

What is it about sand that bothers you so?

Is there any water in here?

No, there's no water. Not until you tell me. We've been at this a long time. You have to tell me, Ben. What is it about sand that bothers you so?

I don't remember.

You do remember.

I don't.

The session dissolved into a similar pattern after that: *You do remember*; *No, I don't*; *Where's the water?* I'd heard it a few times, so I knew. I unwrapped a Clif Bar and popped the earbuds out of my ears.

Ben Dugan leaned down and picked up something off the floor where I couldn't see it. He got up off the chair, holding something in his hand.

"What's he doing now?" I wondered, biting a corner off the chewy bar as if I was watching a movie.

He was facing away from the camera, staring at the wall, gripping some sort of blunt tool. Whatever he held was dripping stringy lines of goo on the floor at his feet. He walked up to the red stenciled numbers and did something I couldn't see.

"What are you doing, Ben Dugan?" I said.

He turned and dropped the tool he'd used on the

floor in front of the camera, and then he was gone. So was the number *1*. It was a wide paintbrush he'd held, slopped with paint.

The *1* had been replaced by a blue blotch, dripping down the wall like cobalt blood.

What did it mean, this blotting out of the number? The whole event had the feeling of a zombie choosing to erase himself from existence.

There, I've marked out my number.

Now I'm ready to face the end.

I switched to M, the main room, and saw that everyone else was sitting on couches and chairs in a far corner. Ben approached, and everyone stood, gathering around him. They appeared to be asking him questions, but it was impossible to know for sure.

"My kingdom for an audio feed," I complained.

Ben started to back away from the rest of the group, and then I saw *him* for the first time. It had to be the person who ran this place, a tall, dark figure at the edge of the screen, barely visible. The figure moved toward Ben, touching him on the shoulder and leading him away. He was speaking to Ben, whispering in his ear: a private message only for the two of them. The whole thing felt haunted, bathed in a black silence.

The two arrived at a door that opened into darkness, and then, just like that, Ben Dugan was gone.

One of the six monitors without controls crackled to life, and I jumped back, tripping over my backpack and falling onto the floor. I'd thought those six were useless, vacant eyes staring back at me without purpose. But now one had come alive in the bomb shelter. I got to my feet and crept in close, staring at a room I'd never seen before.

The first thing that struck me about the room was that it was painted a deep, menacing blue. The floor, the walls, the chair that sat alone—all of it streaked in globs of navy, as if someone had used their bare hands applying the paint.

The second thing that caught my attention was the helmet hanging from the corner of the chair. It was leather, or something like leather; and out of its top rose a series of tubes and wires that hooked into the ceiling. It felt to me as if the room was screaming a message out of the silence: *sit in this chair, put on this helmet, do as I say.* The chair was clearly meant to be sat in, the helmet meant to be put on.

It felt as if I was watching something that wasn't actually happening. Like a video game or a TV show. But I also knew that this wasn't the case—this was real; I knew this kid. I thought seriously about running out of Ms. Goring's bunker, into the woods, and up the path. But there were problems with a plan like that: I was many miles into the wilderness, and I had a notoriously bad sense of direction. I'd barely ever been camping, let alone tried to rough it on my own in the middle of nowhere. What I was seeing scared me, sure, but the prospect of leaving scared me just as much. And the thought of encountering Mrs. Goring or Rainsford as I tried to escape bothered me even more. There was one other, more troubling reason why I stayed and knew I'd keep staying: I was curious. So curious, in fact, that I couldn't stand the idea of not knowing what all this meant or where it would lead. Leaving meant not discovering the truth, which felt unacceptable.

Ben Dugan entered the room. He sat in the chair and held the helmet in his hands, staring at it without moving. He raised his head and said something I couldn't hear; but from the look on his face, I think I got the message.

I can't do this.

He sat a moment longer and then gave in to whatever was happening to him. He slid the helmet on. It covered his head, ears, and eyes, leaving only the lower half of his face exposed.

At least the others will hear him scream, I thought. *They'll come running and save him if things get bad, won't they?*

The tubes jumped grotesquely, as if they had suddenly filled with liquid or electricity, and the screen in the bomb shelter began to fill with data, typed in a glowing green text along the top edge.

Ben Dugan, 15

Acute fear: bugs, spiders, centipedes

Things that crept out of the dirt terrified Ben Dugan. I'd known this all along. The fear had become a looming shadow that ruled his life. It was a miracle he'd made it into the woods at all.

Dr. Stevens's voice filled my mind as I watched the still figure sitting in a blue room.

Now we're getting somewhere, Ben. But why? Why do you fear these things?

I don't know.

You do know.

I don't! Leave me alone!

A blue bar began to move up the right side of the screen, like a thermometer with liquid mercury heating up. Only this mercury was the blackest shade of blue, rising slowly toward the top.

"What the hell is happening to this guy?" I said out loud, wishing Keith was with me and we were back home watching a scary movie.

He's gonna blow! Keith would say, because we'd always do this to calm each other down: yell at the screen until the really bad parts sent us howling through the basement.

The screen glitched and popped, static snow raining down over Ben's sullen figure. His body jerked to life, and suddenly the scene on the screen switched to a child of five or six walking in a park. It was a boy, laughing like little boys do, walking away from whoever was holding the camera. The boy held a small plastic shovel in his hand, waving it like a magic wand as he approached a soggy sandbox. He was in some sort of run-down park, a waning light falling through low clouds.

The image frothed with static again and returned to Ben wearing the helmet. The blue mercury line was rising faster now.

"He's scared," I said.

No kidding! I imagined Keith yelling back.

From this point on, the scene leaped back and forth between Ben Dugan in the blue room and the park setting with the small child. There had to be a screen inside the helmet, a screen that allowed Ben to see what I was seeing. Where the footage came from was a mystery—was it real or made up or somehow pulled out of Ben's brain and projected in front of him?

The kid was in the sandbox now, digging with the plastic shovel. The sand was wet, and the wood rails along the edge of the box were rotting. The boy gave up on the shovel and started digging like a dog, throwing clumps of sodden sand into the camera.

In the room, the blue line neared the top of the screen.

The boy had hold of something heavy and unexpected. He yelled something I couldn't hear. *A dinosaur bone! Mom, look!*

The angle shifted in a way that made my stomach roll, moving in close on what the boy had found.

In the room, the blue line looked as if it was about to

break through the top of the screen and continue up the wall of the bomb shelter. Ben was starting to curl into a ball in the chair.

The boy, who I suddenly understood was a younger version of Ben, had not discovered a dinosaur bone in the sandbox. He lifted the object with great effort, and found that a human finger was in his hand. The finger was attached to an arm, which came out of the sand past the elbow before young Ben Dugan knew what he'd unearthed. The arm was starting to decay, the skin blue and yellow, as if it had been run over by a car and bruised beyond repair. A spider crawled across the arm and reached the boy's finger.

And then things turned ugly.

Little Ben Dugan looked at the camera, his eyes wide with alarm, holding hands with a dead person. The image froze into a photograph of a terrified child, and the screen began to fill with silhouettes of centipedes and spiders, as if they were crawling on the lens of the camera. Every kind of crawling thing darkened the screen, and soon the sandbox was obliterated from view. The park was gone; the sky, too. All that remained in the end were the boy's eyes, white with fear. Everything else was covered by a black swarm of insects.

When the screen returned to the blue room, the blue line had found its end and Ben's neck tightened. The tubes and wires dangled wildly overhead.

And then, all at once, stillness.

He's dead, I thought, staring at the slumped-over body in the chair. *Ben Dugan is dead.*

No, he ain't dead. Just watch, he's coming back.

Shut up, Keith! Leave me alone!

I stood in the bomb shelter by myself, listening to my heart bang against my chest.

A few seconds later the screen powered down, and the blue room vanished from view.

Ben Dugan was gone.

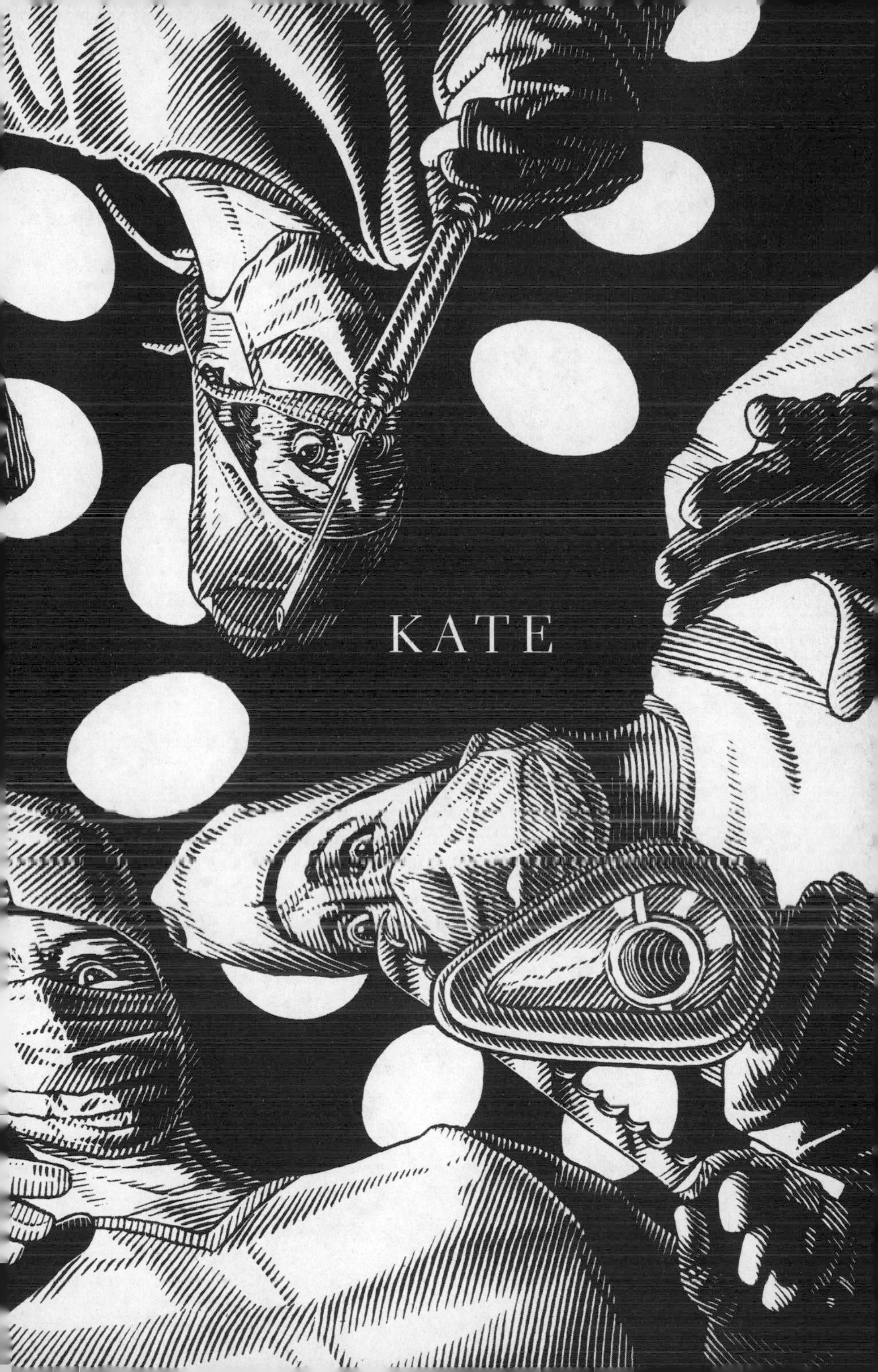

KATE

I needed answers the monitors wouldn't give me. The surveillance system had gone dead, which meant I was both blind and alone. I cycled through the four buttons, but nothing happened. Maybe the monitors were on a timer, or possibly whatever had blown Ben Dugan's mind had also blown a fuse.

A half hour passed in which I tried everything I could think of that might bring the system back online. I searched for loose wires or an access panel, but there were none. I pushed the buttons in every imaginable order on the off chance that I was actually entering a combination that would trigger a restart. I stuck a pencil in the three strange holes made for some kind of audio connection that had gone out of existence decades ago. I even checked the electrical box on the other side of the wall, but everything inside was precaveman era. Touching anything in there, I assumed, would either electrocute me or kill the lights upstairs.

The more I examined the wall of screens, the more the monitors seemed almost alien in their uselessness. I can appreciate old tech, but this was like a dead language or a wheel made of stone: useless to the point of frustration.

Somewhere along the way I became aware of how tired I was. The day had been long and the night longer still, and the strain of hiding out in someone else's basement was starting to wear away my resolve. I devised a half-baked plan in my head, then set the alarm on my watch and slept fitfully for almost four hours, waking at 3:00 AM. When I checked the monitors again, clicking through all the cycles for signs of life, they were still dead. I'd had a plan when I'd reclined on the cot with its decaying springs, but now that the time had come, I wasn't so sure.

I thought about it for several minutes, half asleep on my feet, and decided I could at least go take a look. If things felt wrong, I didn't have to go through with it. I tried to erase all signs of my existence in the room as I put on my backpack. Then I turned out the light and left the bomb shelter.

I walked up the underground tunnel that led into Fort Eden and imagined I was leaving a movie theater in the middle of the show. The only thing missing was a glowing red exit sign. At the end was a door with a bar across the middle, like they'd had in the gymnasium at my grade school. It was the kind of door that could be locked from the outside, but from the inside there was always the bar if you needed to escape from a fire or a violent game of dodge ball.

I was quieter than Mrs. Goring as I went about my business, slowly depressing the bar on the door until it opened, little by little. A crack, nothing more, and I had my first real look at the inside of Fort Eden. All I could see was a black velvet curtain hanging down the wall, covering the barred windows that faced Mrs. Goring's bunker. I pushed the heavy door open a little farther and looked through, finding a single light bathing a round table in the middle of the room. A figure was seated there, reading a book.

Marisa.

If anyone was going to be awake at that hour, I'd known it would be her. I'd half hoped I wouldn't find her so I could look around on my own without fear of being caught, but seeing her there changed my mind. The sound of her voice and the voice of Dr. Stevens drifted through my memory.

It's especially bad at night, when everyone else is asleep.

What happens then?

It's just bad then, like it's so real, you know?

I know. What then? What happens?

First I can't move at all, then I can't get out fast enough. I run down the stairs until I reach the bottom, then I walk to my mom's room and get in bed with her.

You're fifteen, Marisa. I know it's scary, but we should be past this by now.

I know. I'm trying. I just can't.

I didn't want to startle her, so I gathered my courage and whispered as softly as I could.

"Hey, Marisa, it's me."

It was a long way across the great room, and I wasn't

sure if my voice had traveled the entire distance or not. She was stone still. Nothing about Marisa moved.

"It's Will," I whispered, a little louder this time; and her head looked up from the book. She looked noticeably relieved.

"Will?" she said.

"Yeah, Will Besting. From yesterday."

Jeez, Will, get a grip. What other Will could it possibly be?

I opened the door a little bit farther and let it fall against my chest, holding it open. I could go either way now, depending on how this went.

Once she knew it was me, Marisa couldn't get across the open space of the room fast enough. She moved like a gazelle, sliding on her stocking feet. She'd changed into a pair of flannel pajama bottoms, but was still wearing the same T-shirt.

"You scared me half to death," she said, and I felt her breath on my face, warm and soft. She had heard my voice at the start. I realized I must have startled her. I felt guilty for making her feel that way.

"I'm sorry. I didn't mean to scare you."

"It's okay. I scare easily at night. And I have insomnia. Bad combo."

She must have been able to tell I was afraid, too. Maybe I was even backing away, making my retreat for the bomb shelter. Her voice was calm, soothing almost, and she was reaching her hand out toward me as if I was a scared dog that she was trying to reason with.

"Come on, it's okay, Will. No one else is awake."

I stepped through the doorway, the faint light over the table drawing my eyes.

"Better leave something to block the door," she whispered. "It doesn't open from this side. I've tried."

She looked at me curiously, like she wanted to ask what was down the long corridor and how I'd come to find the other side of the door, but she didn't ask. I took off my shoes, setting one on the floor at the doorjamb, and I let the door swing next to it. I was inside Fort Eden, someplace I'd promised myself I would never go.

"Over here," she said, taking my hand and guiding me to the right, away from the round table and the faint light. She wasn't holding my hand so much as dragging me forward like a little kid through a grocery store, and when we reached a grouping of furniture, she let go. I looked at the ceiling as we went, trying to find a surveillance camera, but there was hardly any light to see by. There was something about this corner that seemed important from the start: it was out of range of the view I'd seen in Mrs. Goring's basement. We were hidden from whatever camera fed into the bomb shelter monitor.

She pointed back in the direction from which we'd come.

"Everyone is sleeping down there, at the other end. Plus the doors are solid and heavy in this place. I'm not sure they'd hear us if we screamed."

"Let's not find out," I said, my eyes following the direction she pointed. I saw three doors along one wall.

"The one on the left is for the girls, on the right is for the boys," she said, and I imaged beds and a bathroom on either side, like little dorm rooms.

"What about the middle door? Where's that one go?" I asked.

She sat on a leather couch, ignoring my question, and I noticed the book in her hand but didn't ask what it was. Everything was smothered in shadows, but I took note of what I saw as best I could. I wanted to know this place, to map it out if I could.

"It's big in here," I said, sitting down at the other end of the couch, not wanting to scare her away.

"Will," she said, leaning in a little closer. "How did

you end up on the other side of that door?"

My throat turned dry, so dry, in fact, that I didn't think I'd have a voice if I tried to speak again. I pulled off my pack and cracked open a bottle of water, holding it out to her.

"No thanks."

Two quick sips, then the cap went back on. Where to begin?

"There's another building, I'm in there."

"You mean Mrs. Goring's place?"

"Yeah, there's a basement. I'm staying in the basement."

"But how—"

She seemed to add up things in her head, to imagine how I might have arrived there, and her voice died in the shadows.

"I'm fine," I said, not knowing how much I should say. "It's dry. Better than staying in the woods."

I had questions, many of them, but one in particular I didn't know how to ask.

Is Ben Dugan dead?

If I asked the question she would know I could see things, and that would lead to more questions I didn't want to answer. Not yet anyway.

"What's he like?" I asked instead.

"Who?"

"You know, the main guy Dr. Stevens told us about. The doctor."

"He's not what I expected," she pondered. "I mean, he's fine. I actually think you'd like him."

"Really?"

"He came up those stairs after Mrs. Goring left. That part was kind of weird."

Marisa pointed to a rectangular hole in the floor—I could only see the first two steps. They were in the middle of the room, going down into black. "Even Kate was scared when he first showed up. You know how there are all those old movies where a beautiful girl comes down the stairs in her prom dress or whatever? This was like the opposite. It was like he came up out of the ground."

"I thought you said I'd like him."

"You would. After that he came to the table and told us all to sit down. Then he said his name was Rainsford, but more than that. He was like, '*You will be tempted to call me many things—Doctor, Mister, Sir, the old man of the house. Please, just Rainsford.*' After that it was cool. Just hearing his voice made us all like him."

Until he killed Ben Dugan, I wanted to say.

"What then, after that?"

"You've got a lot of questions."

"It's boring in the basement."

"Then come back. He asked about you."

She leaned a little closer; her brown eyes turned black in the darkness. "I think he can help us."

"Why do you say that?"

"Because. He cured Ben. This guy is for real."

"Cured Ben? But that's not what happened. Ben's dead."

Marisa pulled back, as if the scared little dog she'd coaxed out of the wild was about to bite her.

"Ben's not dead. He's fine."

She pointed to the middle door on the far wall, the one between the rooms for the girls and the boys. "He went through that door, and when he came back, he wasn't afraid anymore."

She looked at me warily, as if she wasn't sure I could be trusted. "What are you not telling me?"

I took another drink of water and felt my throat struggle to choke it down. This wasn't going the way I'd imagined it. I barely knew Marisa. What if she'd been turned against me in my absence? So it surprised me when I revealed so much, so quickly.

"I found a room downstairs, in the basement of Mrs. Goring's place. It's an old bomb shelter, or maybe it's like one of those places you go so you can see what the enemy's doing when they show up and take over a fort. You know, to plan a counterattack or something."

Marisa had moved as far away from me as she could without falling off the couch. She was looking at me, figuring things out. She was a real thinker, this girl.

"Are you *watching* us, Will?"

I paused, a feeling in my gut that I'd said more than I should have.

"It's not like I found it on purpose or anything. The monitors were just *there*. And anyway, I can't see hardly anything."

Marisa didn't speak, so I charged ahead. "This big room with the table, I can see it sometimes. And there are two other rooms; they're like confessionals or something. And the room Ben went into. I saw where he went, and it's not what you think. I thought he was dead."

Marisa stared at me for a long time: ten seconds, maybe more.

"What did you see?" she finally asked.

I told her about the helmet and the creepy blue walls, but I stopped short of describing the bizarre images that filled the screen.

Marisa shook her head. "All I know is that when he came back, he wasn't afraid of bugs and spiders anymore. But that is a little creepy, the helmet thing. I wonder what it does?"

Part of me wanted to yell, *It scares you to death!* But there was another part that said, *Don't do it; leave it alone*. I was starting to doubt myself. Ben Dugan wasn't dead; and what was more, he was cured, or at least Marisa believed he was. Ben Dugan wasn't afraid anymore. I envied him that, and I knew what Marisa feared. If she understood that the treatment would put her face-to-face with those fears, she'd never go through with it. As crazy as Fort Eden was, I couldn't shake the feeling that I might be robbing her of a cure.

"How did you know what Ben was afraid of?" I asked.

"Rainsford made us tell."

"What do you mean, *made* you tell?"

"That's not right—I meant he *got us* to tell. He's a very persuasive guy that way. Everyone told, all but one."

I could see them, sitting in a circle at the table under some kind of twisted spell, spilling what they knew. And I also knew that of the six, there was one who would never say what she feared.

"Avery," I said—another mistake. How should I know

who would and wouldn't tell?

"Yeah, Avery." Marisa didn't skip a beat; and what was even better, she moved closer to me on the couch again. "She's *so* quiet, right? But I'm starting to think it's more than that. She said something about when it was her turn that gave me the chills."

I knew what Avery had said. I'd heard her say it a dozen times already.

You can't cure me. No one can.

I asked Marisa what she thought Avery was afraid of. She shrugged, turning quiet and thoughtful, so I went back to Ben Dugan.

"Ben went into a room and talked for a while, but I couldn't hear him. That's something I didn't mention before. I can only see some things. I can't hear anything at all. There's no audio for the monitors."

"So they're like security cameras," Marisa said, and she seemed to mellow about them, her concern turning to intrigue. I couldn't hear what people were saying, so it was at least 50 percent less intrusive. "I bet the room you saw was where we can go to talk to Dr. Stevens. There's one on each side in the back, one for girls and one for boys."

"Whoa, hold on. Are you saying Dr. Stevens was talking to Ben?"

"Yeah, she's there if we need her. We can go in there and talk about how we're doing. Ben did that before he got cured."

"But she's not here. She left."

"I don't mean she's *in* the room. It's a monitor. She's back home. We call; she answers. At least that's how it's supposed to work. I haven't tried it."

My eyes had adjusted to the dim light, and I asked her about the other rooms in Fort Eden. She said that there was a study on the far side of the stairs, but the door was always locked. Behind us was a library, which reminded me of the book she had set on the floor.

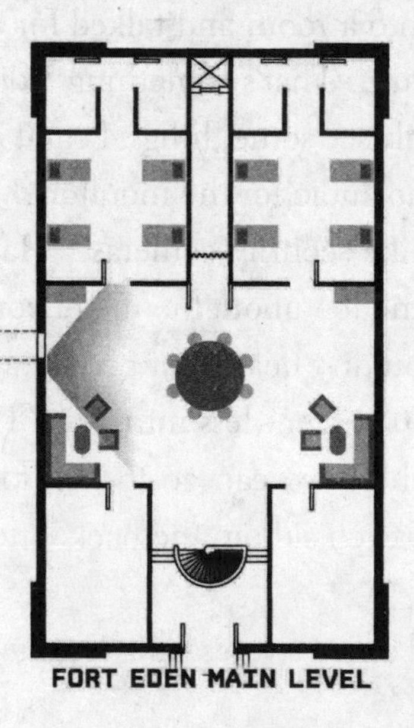
FORT EDEN MAIN LEVEL

"What are you reading?" I asked.

She picked it up and handed it to me. Now both of my hands were full, one with a water bottle and one with a book. If she'd wanted to hold my hand she couldn't.

"*The Pearl*," I said. "Pretty good book."

"Yeah well, we're all being forced to read it, so I hope you're right."

"Wait, you're *all* reading *The Pearl*? What for?"

Marisa shrugged. "Rainsford put a box in the middle of the table and asked us to put all our electronics inside, including phones. Not like we were getting a signal, but it was hard. It reminded me of this youth group I used to go to. We'd show up, and this twenty-something youth pastor would pass around a cardboard box asking for phones, which he promised to return at the end of the night. By the time he got it back, that box was overflowing. Anyway, Rainsford said it would bond us, reading the same book."

In the back of my mind I was thinking, Why *The Pearl*? But instead, I said something really stupid.

"I read it once before. I think you'll like it."

I'd already made this mistake before, making it seem as if I was something special. *Why of course I've read it; Steinbeck and Hemingway are my homeboys.*

Marisa didn't reply. She snatched the book out of my hand and turned to the side, staring at the cover instead of staring at me. Then she said something I was completely unprepared for.

"Tell me what you're afraid of, Will."

The question came out of nowhere, and it rang in my ears like a shot from a cannon. Marisa turned to me again. "Everyone here is afraid. *Really* afraid. It's why we're here. The first part of the cure is telling. Everyone told but you."

"Avery didn't tell."

Marisa looked off toward the dim light over the table once more and got up to leave.

"Forget it."

I wanted her to stay more than anything I'd ever wanted in my life. I wanted our secret night to never end.

"I'll tell you another secret, but not that one. Not yet."

She stopped, turned, sat down. I'd piqued her interest, but she was leery, I could tell, as if I was about to trick her. At least she was back.

"Shoot."

I took a deep breath and looked her right in the eye.

"I don't go to a private school. I'm homeschooled."

"Really? Why?"

"Because me and school don't exactly get along."

Not a huge confession, but it was something, and it was enough.

"Does it have something to do with what you're afraid of?"

"Maybe."

She reached out for the water bottle and I handed it to her, looking at her shirt as her eyes tilted back to the ceiling.

I WANNA BE ADORED.

The dream I'd had flashed before my eyes—her body on the gurney—and for an instant my mind blazed with fear. It was a strange feeling, like someone had put it there for me to find and I'd stumbled onto it.

"The Stone Roses," I said.

"No way." She smiled, moved a little closer. "You knew?"

"It's a great song. Who wouldn't know?"

I Wanna Be Adored wasn't a statement about Marisa; it was a '90s song by a British band called The Stone Roses.

I wished more than anything that I'd really known this about her, that I'd seen her for the first time and known, because we shared a common interest in something obscure. But you do what you have to do in order to win the girl, at least that's what my dad keeps telling me. I knew because she wore the shirt when she met with Dr. Stevens.

I knew because I'd already heard Marisa tell me.

We agreed not to say anything to anyone, at least for one more day. She wouldn't reveal where I was hiding or that I could see certain things. She made me promise not to watch if she went into the room to talk with Dr. Stevens, and I made her promise not to rat me out. At least not yet.

"I think you should come back," she said at the door. "But you're right, too. When Ben came back, he said the joints in his fingers hurt. He kept flexing his fists. He was really psyched, and he swore we could put a spider in his sheets and he wouldn't even care; but there's no doubt this place isn't normal."

"No kidding," I said. "See you tomorrow night? Same time, same place?"

She smiled shyly, looked at *The Pearl*, then back at me.

"It's a date. And bring your fear. You tell me yours; I'll tell you mine."

It wasn't exactly fair that I knew everything about her, but I was a retro-video-game air hockey master who didn't attend a real school. I needed every advantage I could get.

The door closed behind me, and I started the long walk down the corridor alone. The lightness in my step felt heavier the deeper I went, until, entering the basement, I felt like I was carrying a coffin on my back.

The basement lights were on. Had I left them on? I couldn't remember.

I glanced around the corner of the corridor and found that I was not alone.

Mrs. Goring had entered the basement while I was gone.

I made an unfortunate sound—a half scream—before I could shut my stupid mouth. Then I backed up, and my arm connected with the corner of the doorjamb. My funny bone went berserk, an electric tingle pulsing down my arm.

I stood in the darkened corridor rubbing the sting out of my elbow, trying to think . . . *Could I take the old lady or not? Maybe I could make it to a shelf and beat her back with a can of corn.*

A few seconds later I had a feeling in my bones that Mrs. Goring was stalking me. It was quiet in the basement, too quiet; and I imagined her carrying a baseball bat or a rolling pin, inching her way toward the corridor.

I should have run up the hall into Fort Eden, but something told me that this was an even worse idea than waiting to be clobbered by a heavy wooden object. My head started to clear, and reason returned. Whoever was in there might not know that I was down here with them. Was that possible? I had been careful not to leave any trace of evidence. Maybe Mrs. Goring was hard of hearing.

There was movement around the corner, which sounded like someone loading a cart with cans and boxes. I looked at my watch. 5:10 AM. I'd been upstairs in the fort longer than I should have been. Morning had come to the clearing, and Mrs. Goring was gathering supplies to make breakfast for the visitors. That was her job, after all; but why hadn't she heard my intrusion?

I risked a quick look, petrified that it would be my

last, and there she was, doing just what I'd presumed: filling up the cart with pancake mix, canned peaches, a jar of peanut butter, a plastic jug of syrup. Seeing the trappings of what would be a spectacular breakfast I would not enjoy made my mouth water. But it was okay, because I also heard then why she hadn't found me. Mrs. Goring was humming—a pair of small headphones stuck to her ears—quietly butchering some song in her head.

The door to the corridor sat ajar by a foot, and I watched as she turned to leave with her supplies, her eyes falling in my direction. I stepped softly back on the slick concrete, and the cart moved toward me, the bad wheel wobbling loudly. She pushed the cart up the hall, then stopped and slammed the door shut behind her, sealing me inside.

I listened to Mrs. Goring drive the cart away and round the corner, heard it bouncing over my head up the path that led to the kitchen. My stomach rumbled, empty and searching for pancakes; but at least I had safely avoided being discovered.

Soon I was back in the bomb shelter, sitting on the cot and wishing Marisa was with me. I opened a Clif Bar and choked it down with water. Looking in my bag and seeing so many more, I wished I'd packed something else. The lack of variety was already sending my taste buds into a death spiral.

Boredom sunk in rapidly. I was too cautious now to listen to my Recorder; Mrs. Goring had taught me better. Getting lost in an audio world of my own would present its own set of risks as long as people were awake and moving around. Listening had to be worth it.

I could record, though, and this I did, keeping my voice low as I described everything that had happened to me. After a time my eyes fell on the two paperbacks. I was not, generally speaking, a reader. I was a listener. Audio diaries were of particular interest. People are always talking about how important it is to write things down, but I think recording your own voice is more important. I've tried to read many biographies; most of them die on the page. Reading Martin Luther King's story is wholly unsatisfying, but if I listen to him speak I feel like I understand who he was. Or, better yet, listening to someone nobody's ever heard of. There is nothing I like more than hearing average people tell their own stories.

Still, I was bored and there were these books in what had become my home away from home, so I picked each of them up. I should not have been surprised to find *The Pearl* among them, but I was. The other book was called *The Woman in the Dunes* by a Japanese writer whose name I couldn't pronounce. Both books were tattered and yellow at the edges, with pencil markings that had all but faded away on some of the pages.

I fell back on the cot and began reading. It made me happy—imagining Marisa as she read, wondering what page she was on as I read the same words. It was something we could talk about, something shared and real.

I grew drowsy, and turning off the light, slept for a few hours, the darkness making the basement like a tomb where time had no meaning, until I was abruptly awakened by a light dancing before my eyes.

The wall was alive again, the center monitor crackling to life. I got up and spun the dimmer switch on, filling the room with a harsh light. I could see the main room of Fort Eden again, buzzing with activity. Everyone was awake, and checking my watch, I realized I'd slept a full four hours. It was almost 9:00 AM.

Marisa sat alone in a corner on a couch, reading. I couldn't help wondering what page she was on. Kate and Ben were cross-legged on the floor, talking to each other. I had to admit that Ben Dugan looked not only fine, but his body language spoke of a contented, healthy guy. He wore a T-shirt I hadn't seen before with some sort of emblem on it. I couldn't hear what they were saying, but it looked as if Kate was grilling him for information. I found it interesting that Connor, who had been inseparable from Kate from the start, kept glancing their way from his place at the table, where he was aimlessly fanning a paperback. Alex sat at the table, too, drawing in a notebook.

There was one person missing; but by cycling the monitor to G—the room with the numbers 2, 5, and 7 stenciled on the back wall—I found her.

Avery Varone, the girl with many foster homes. She was staring right at me, saying nothing at all. It matched what I already knew perfectly, and I risked putting in my earbuds and dialing up one of her audio sessions.

Nothing's going to change if you can't be honest with me.

I know.

I understand that you're afraid, really I do. Can you tell me anything, anything at all?

You can't help me.

Well, I don't know about that. I've been doing this

awhile. I've helped many people. I think I can help you, if you'll trust me.

Uh-huh.

Just think about it, okay? The first step is the truth. We're sort of stuck until we get there.

Right.

What was Avery thinking now, in the strange room, as she stared at me? I knew she couldn't see me, but she looked vacant and afraid, as if she was watching a ghost hover before her eyes. She was a pretty girl—long brown hair and a sweet face—but seeing her then and hearing her voice in my ears, I was overcome by her hopelessness. How different would she look if she could be cured?

Cured, made unafraid. But of what or of whom? That was the unanswerable question about Avery Varone.

Even I didn't know because, in all those sessions, she'd never told.

I knew Mrs. Goring would leave with the food eventually. She was smart to wait until after 9:00 AM, when teenagers were both awake and famished. I heard the cart heading down from upstairs and felt the power of the basement door bursting open.

I'd already decided what I was going to do before the rattling cart showed up, and I was out of the bomb shelter before Mrs. Goring reached the top of the corridor on her way to Fort Eden. I started up the ramp, waiting for the door to close partway once more. When it did, I ran the entire distance, standing in the shadow of the incline, listening and recording.

Everyone had gathered around as Mrs. Goring slapped their hands away from the cart.

"Breakfast will be served at the table, not a second sooner. This isn't a zoo."

"Oh, come on, we're starving," Connor protested. He was the biggest, so it stood to reason he'd be the hungriest.

"Out of my way or I'll ram you with the cart."

I couldn't risk sticking my head through the doorway, so I wasn't able to see what was happening. Apparently Connor had been blocking the way but had moved, laughing loudly.

"You're funny, Mrs. Goring."

"Watch yourself, Connor," Alex said, jumping in.

"She might bust your knee with a frying pan."

"We appreciate the food, Mrs. Goring. Pay no attention to these Neanderthals," Kate said. She was perplexingly kind, a teacher's pet attitude having overcome her.

"I'll get Avery," Marisa said. I couldn't see her, either, until she reached the door to the girls' quarters and I caught a glimpse of her through the six-inch opening in the door.

After that it was all banter at the breakfast table and Mrs. Goring telling them to make their beds and flush the toilets. Marisa returned with Avery in tow and joined the group, all of them sitting around the table.

"How'd it go with the doc?" Kate asked. It was mildly insensitive, but coming from Kate, par for the course.

"Fine."

"I feel sorry for her," Ben said. "Up all hours talking to us. It's kind of amazing what she's doing. It's like twenty-four hours on call."

I had to agree. However Dr. Stevens was being piped into Fort Eden, she probably wasn't getting a lot of sleep. I could imagine her in her office back home, webcam at the ready. They must have the place hardwired to an underground connection somewhere, because there sure wasn't a signal hanging around in the air.

"Where's Rainsford? When will we see him again?" asked Ben. "I'd like to thank him."

"I bet you would," said Mrs. Goring. She was somewhere across the room, pulling open curtains. "He's got a lot of work to do, so don't bother him."

"What kind of work?" asked Ben.

"The kind that fixes messed-up kids like you; what other kind is there?"

Wow, Mrs. Goring was in a real mood this morning. I was halfway glad I didn't have to deal with her, although the pancakes smelled amazing and I wished for a tall stack, covered in peanut butter and syrup.

There was a loud clang and I jumped back, thinking for a brief second that someone was hitting the door I stood next to. But it was someone outside trying to get in.

"Who in blazes is that?" said Mrs. Goring. I heard her stomping across the room in her boots while everyone else went silent. The door clanged again, like it was being hit with a hammer.

"Whoever you are, if you're kicking that door with the toe of your boot, I'll have your hide!" she yelled.

A few people laughed softly, but a silent curiosity had overtaken the group inside the fort. When the door flew open, the quiet was broken by the sound of a voice I hadn't heard before.

"Hello, Mrs. Goring. I smelled the pancakes."

"Like hell you did."

Whoever it was laughed—a nice laugh, come to think of it—and entered the fort.

"It's been a long time, Davis. I trust you're feeling well."

"Oh yes, very well."

Who the heck was Davis?

"It won't last if I have anything to say about it." Mrs. Goring was being incredibly rude, but that was her way; and whoever this Davis character was, he didn't seem to mind.

"This must be them," he said, entering the room as the door was closed.

"Well, of course it's them. Didn't you learn anything when you were here?"

"Oh, I learned plenty, Mrs. Goring."

A stillness, then he spoke again.

"If it's okay, I'll join you. I'm Davis."

He sat, or so it seemed, and greetings were exchanged as they ate. Whoever he was, the girls seemed particularly nervous about his arrival.

"Rainsford called me, asked if I'd stay on for a few days and help Mrs. Goring fix the pump down at the pond. That old thing is always going out."

I knew about the pond but hadn't thought much of it until then.

"How do you know him?" asked Kate, an air of flirtation in her voice that I hadn't even heard with Connor. This Davis guy, I thought, must be a real stud.

"Well, that's the other reason I'm here. To encourage you."

"How so?" Avery, the quiet one, had spoken to a total stranger.

"I'm a graduate of the program," Davis said, then it sounded as if he'd stuffed a wad of pancakes in his mouth.

"No way," Connor said, slapping his own knee or Davis's back, I couldn't tell which. "What were you afraid of?"

"Mrs. Goring."

Everyone laughed, and this time I was pretty sure of what I heard: Mrs. Goring slapping Davis on the arm, and Davis laughing with everyone else.

I felt really lonely all of a sudden, like I'd been left unpicked on the playground.

"I couldn't stand the pond when I showed up here," he said. "I hated it."

"Because you're afraid of fish?" Connor said, and got a laugh from Ben and Alex.

"I'll take a hamburger over fish sticks any day, but I wasn't afraid of fish. I was afraid of water. Couldn't even drink the stuff. I know, weird, right?"

"Yeah, totally," said Alex, but Avery came to Davis's rescue.

"I don't think it's so strange. You're afraid of dogs. What's the difference?"

"A dog can kill you," Alex said. He hadn't liked being called out.

"Did you know that a person can drown in a teaspoon of water?" Davis asked.

"Really?" Kate said.

There was a pause; maybe Davis was wiping his mouth with a napkin.

"No, not really," he said. "Before I came here though, I thought stuff like that was true. As far as I was concerned, the shower could kill me. I didn't smell too good back then."

"I find that hard to imagine," said Kate.

"Yeah," said Avery. The competition was on; even I

could tell that much, and I couldn't even see what this guy looked like.

"You must be Ben," Davis again. "I can tell by your shirt. You earned it, man; wear it proudly."

"Thanks. How old are you?" Ben Dugan asked. "When were you here?"

"Seventeen. I was here the same as you, when I was your age. You're all fifteen, right?"

Nothing, so everyone must be nodding. A chair was pushed back, and someone moved away from the table.

"Thank you, Mrs. Goring. That was perfect."

It was Marisa, finished with her breakfast.

"Sure it was," Mrs. Goring replied sourly.

"So here's the deal," Davis went on. He'd gained their confidence, and mine, too. "Rainsford told me Ben was cured, and I'm here to tell you I've been cured, too. Later today, when the sun warms things up, I'll be diving in the pond searching for a busted pipe. I want you all to hear me now. This program works when nothing else does. I'll be around this week. If you have questions, don't hesitate to ask. I owe my life to this place, so it's the least I can do."

"I'm going as soon as he'll let me," Kate said. "I might want to talk about it."

Yeah, I bet you would, I thought.

I'd let myself get all comfortable, not paying nearly enough attention; and all at once someone was standing where I could see them through the crack in the door. The person was next to the black curtain, pulling it open.

"What did I tell you about touching things you don't need to be touching?" Mrs. Goring shouted. I looked down the side of the wall, and there was Marisa, staring back at me. As the curtain came open, she tossed a note through the crack in the door.

"Sorry, Mrs. Goring," she said, walking toward her. "It's just so nice to have some light in here."

"That's it; breakfast is over. Pile everything on the cart," Mrs. Goring said.

"Way to go, Marisa," Connor joked. I got the feeling he and the other boys were grabbing pancakes, stuffing them in their mouths, until Davis's voice filled the room again.

"There's one other thing," he said, almost shyly, I thought. "One of you is missing. Rainsford would like me to find him. I know the woods pretty well."

"Will Besting," Marisa said, her voice betraying at least a little worry.

"Yeah, Will Besting," said Davis. "If any of you hears

anything, I'd appreciate it if you'd tell me. There's nothing to worry about, no bears around here. But he needs help, and this place can help him. I think if I could talk to him, he might come in on his own."

Great. That's all I needed. Some seventeen-year-old pretty boy trying to track me down.

I started for the bomb shelter, clutching Marisa's note in my hand, hoping Davis wouldn't search Mrs. Goring's basement anytime soon.

I'll visit Dr. Stevens when everyone is asleep. That's how you'll know. Come see me then, okay? Marisa.

The last time I'd gotten a note like Marisa's was in the fourth grade. I even remember what it said.

Meet me downstairs by the water fountain after school. I have something for you. Jennifer

Jennifer never showed up, but Marisa would. She didn't have anyplace else to go, and she'd be awake. I wasn't a night owl like she was, and I definitely didn't have insomnia. I slept just fine, and as often as possible. But my biggest worry wasn't that I'd fall asleep; I was more concerned that the system would fail again. I'd miss her signal when the time came and stand her up, like Jennifer had stood me up at the water fountain.

Looks like someone's got a date. Keith's voice rattled in my head, and I imagined him leaning against the doorjamb in my room wearing that goofy green baseball cap. *Don't blow it.*

Don't worry, Keith, I won't, I thought. But I was nervous just the same, and reminded myself to read some of *The Pearl* so Marisa and I would have something to talk about. I turned off the monitor in case it was on a timer and only stayed on for so many hours a day. If that was true, how was I going to keep an eye on the room where Marisa would give me the signal? The whole situation was starting to stress me out big-time, so I reclined on the cot and started reading. I'd heard *The Pearl* on tape a long time ago, in my parents' car, I think, but I couldn't really remember it.

An hour later I turned the monitor back on and saw that the main room at Fort Eden was empty.

"Weird," I said. "Where is everyone?"

I looked at my watch—nearly 11:00 AM—then back

at the monitor, cycling through the three rooms I had access to. The whole place felt deserted, until Mrs. Goring came into view. She was on the farthest end of the main room, walking into the girls' quarters.

"What's she doing in there?" I wondered. The door to the girls' quarters closed, and Mrs. Goring was gone. For a few seconds I thought nothing of it. She was in there changing the sheets or something. What else would she be doing in there? But then I had a hunch, a sort of cold feeling up the back of my neck, and I clicked the white G button, bringing up the room where the girls went to talk to Dr. Stevens.

The chair sat empty. The stencils of 2, 5, and 7 were still there on the wall. I wasn't prepared a second later when Mrs. Goring sat down, and even less prepared because of the way she did it: fast and close. She sat right up next to the monitor screen, creating a fish-eye effect in the lens. It was as if she didn't understand how it worked, staring grotesquely into the monitor, her eyes darting back and forth, a fist of knuckles banging on the screen. And she was yelling. If I had to guess, I would have said she was yelling for Dr. Stevens to come out, as if Dr. Stevens lived in the monitor itself and needed to be woken up.

How old was Mrs. Goring, that she couldn't grasp such things? Seventy-five? Eighty-five? Older still? Maybe she'd just lived in the woods too long, losing touch with reality.

Mrs. Goring settled back and began talking in short bursts. I'd have gladly given up my air hockey table and my Atari and my little brother, Keith, in exchange for audio. What was she saying, and why was she saying it? What possible reason could there be for Mrs. Goring to talk with Dr. Stevens?

I cycled back to the main room in Fort Eden, which remained empty. Everyone was gone, and it was starting to really bother me. Were they in the basement of the fort, having a round of shock therapy? I'm not sure what caused me to think what I thought next. It could have been that I was sick and tired of the oppressive silence of the basement. Or maybe I'd come to feel so alone and afraid that something deep inside finally snapped. Could have been that I wanted to see Marisa, even if I couldn't talk to her. All I remember is that I had a thought that led me out the door of the bomb shelter.

If I could get into this basement once, I could do it again.

One last look at Mrs. Goring sitting in the room.

She's there. I can make it.

I turned off the monitor and put on my backpack, and before I knew it I was up the long ramp to Fort Eden and standing in the main room. Still empty, but I could hear Mrs. Goring moving in the girls' quarters, where the door stood slightly ajar. Her hand would be on the door before I could get out. What would she do if she saw me standing there? She'd think I was crazy. Did she carry a pistol tucked in her jeans? The thoughts that crossed my mind of a bloody mess in Fort Eden had the effect of freezing me in place; and before I could get myself moving again, Mrs. Goring was pulling the door all the way open, about to walk back into the main room.

My only chance was the stairway leading down, the one on which Rainsford had appeared. A metal railing went around three sides, but I was on the open end—a small piece of good luck. I bolted, hit the first stair with my heel, and immediately had second thoughts. The stairs were narrow and stunningly steep; but worse than that, a thick smear of darkness obliterated all light after a few feet. I lost my footing and slid down four or five steps, my backpack bouncing as I searched for a railing. The way was turning rapidly—a spiral stone staircase—and, catching my foot on a step, I came to a bone-rattling halt.

I lay faceup, staring into the murky light of Fort Eden. I looked down, and the descent felt alive and menacing, like the open mouth of a beast with teeth of bared stone.

What is this place?

One thing was clear: the basement to Fort Eden was deep in the ground. How deep, I had no idea. Hidden where I was, it wasn't hard to imagine how the winding stairs, steep and crumbling with age, might go on forever.

Mrs. Goring's boots banged on the floor until she got to the opening below which I was hidden, and then she stopped.

"Stupid kids can't keep their hands off anything. No more syrup."

She was mopping the metal railing around the opening with a wet rag. From where I lay, it looked as if she was seeing right through me, the silhouette of her bulbous head outlined against the light. A few seconds passed, then she was moving off again, forward toward the library.

It wasn't until I tried to get up that I realized why Mrs. Goring hadn't taken notice of a kid on the stairs. I'd thought I'd fallen four or five steps, but this thing was almost as steep as a ladder. I'd fallen ten steps or more, deep into the gloom, and I hadn't seen any sign of the bottom.

I have to tell Marisa. I have to tell them all.

Just as quickly as I had this thought, I had another.

How could they not know about this ghastly stairway?

It was impossible to imagine Connor Bloom not goading the rest of the guys into trying to climb down. He was the captain of the football team, so it would be his job to push everyone to the limit. He'd have dared Ben and Alex to go deeper and deeper. They knew, and yet they stayed. On top of that, it was stupidly dangerous. What if someone fell into the hole? What then? Something didn't add up.

I took out my penlight and clicked it on, pointing its meager beam farther down the stairs. A secret part of me had wanted to go deeper, to see how far it went and what was at the bottom. But that feeling passed in an instant as the darkness devoured my little light. A chill enveloped me. Was there no end to the depth of Fort Eden?

I climbed up the stairs just far enough to peer into the room. Mrs. Goring was in the library, where I could hear her mumbling and moving books. *Now's my chance*, I thought, and climbed the rest of the way out, standing at the edge of the opening. The weight of my pack was pulling me off balance, like it was part of a plot that involved me tumbling down an endless, winding staircase. I felt as if I was suffocating. I needed air, *real* air, not the dank stuff of a bomb shelter.

Crossing the room, I opened the main door as quietly as I could. Seeing no one, I ran through the clearing and into the trees. The rain had stopped and the sun was up, a warm day rapidly blooming. I knew it would turn bitter cold by nightfall, but for now I was free of Fort Eden and Mrs. Goring's basement, filling my lungs with mountain air.

It was a short walk to the pond, not more than five minutes, where I heard voices bouncing off the water. Connor, Ben, and Alex were horsing around at the water's edge, but no one had taken the plunge. The girls sat together on a dock, their feet dangling in the frigid water. There were long limbs from mossy trees scattered over the pond, which wasn't very big. I was sure I could throw a rock from one side to the other if I tried.

"He can stay down there a hell of a long time,"

Connor said to the girls. They all chose to ignore him. They were looking off to the left, and from my position in the trees, I could see that they were staring at a small shed that sat on stilts over the water's edge.

A body burst out of the pond, grabbing hold of one of the beams supporting the small structure, gasping for air. In his other hand he held a pipe wrench.

"Seventy-four seconds," Avery said, looking at her watch, then at Marisa.

"Not bad!" Kate yelled across the pond.

It was Davis who had been underwater, but now he'd climbed onto the small landing in front of the shed. I guessed it was the pump house.

Davis was everything I wasn't, and I was glad Kate and Avery were fighting for his attention. It left less room for Marisa, and I didn't stand a chance against this guy. He was tall with dark hair, and muscular in a way I could only dream of. A straight, gladiator nose sat flawlessly beneath dark eyes. He flashed a smile at the girls, then ducked into the pump house and started banging the pipe wrench against something I couldn't see.

"This guy's a real player," I whispered to myself, pushing branches away from my face so I could see more of the pond.

Avery surprised everyone by diving off the dock. She stayed under until she, too, reached the pump house and emerged breathless, reaching up her hand until Davis pulled her free of the frosty water. The two of them laughed, Kate stewed, Marisa peered into the forest. Connor pushed Ben into the pond, and it was game on for the guys, which I was very happy not to participate in. Still, the whole thing was like a scene from summer camp. Hanging by the water, flirting, horsing around, laughing. I felt alone as I so often did, the trees pressing in against me like they were my only friends in the world.

After a time Kate called to Davis.

"I'm ready now. I need to talk to you first though."

I thought of how stupid I'd been. What made me think these cures would only occur at night? What if one of the monitors in the bomb shelter turned on and I missed it?

Davis had on one of those diver watches, and after looking at it, he stood. He said something to Avery I couldn't hear and she blushed, then he dove back into the pond, resurfacing at the dock twenty or so seconds later.

"I need to be back in the city by three," he said,

wiping a wet hand down his face. "With the path and the bad road, it's a couple hours."

"I thought you were staying with us," Kate complained. It was after noon, which meant Davis would only be around another hour at most. I got the feeling he hadn't tried searching for me as he'd said he would. He seemed more interested in Avery and in fixing whatever was wrong with the pump.

"No can do. But I'll be back tomorrow morning; you can count on it. I'm on the case until the pump is fixed and Will Besting is found."

Good luck. Ain't gonna happen.

He climbed out of the water and took a towel from a stack on the dock, then his feet were in a pair of flip-flops and he was walking with Kate. They were coming toward me and I got nervous, ducking farther into the brush and the trees. It was because of this that I only heard bits and pieces of their conversation as they walked past. Something about a job he had in Los Angeles, working in food services for a film crew that made straight-to-video horror flicks. A lot of night shooting and the zombies got hungry, or something like that, followed by laughter. I stayed behind them as they made their way on the path back to the fort.

I went deeper in the woods to their left. Their voices grew quieter. When they reached Fort Eden, they sat on the steps and spoke so quietly that I couldn't hear what they were saying. I moved off into the trees, and snapped a twig, which Kate didn't seem to notice but Davis did. He got up, stared in my general direction, and spoke.

"Will, if you're out there, you should come in. We all want you here. And you know it's going to get cold again tonight."

I didn't move a muscle, didn't even breathe. If Davis came into the woods, he'd surely find me in no time flat.

"Come on, Will. It's okay."

Kate pulled on the towel around Davis's neck, and he sat again. I thought I heard her say something about me being able to take care of myself, but I couldn't be sure. Everyone else came bounding up the path, the outdoors having put them all in a good mood. A few minutes of small talk at the entryway, then the door opened and Mrs. Goring's voice filled the clearing.

"Lunch. Now."

She disappeared inside, and everyone followed. Davis was the last to go in; but before he did, he turned and stared into the trees.

He knew I was there. I could tell. Tomorrow he would come looking for me, but it would be too late.

I'd already be gone.

The door to Mrs. Goring's bunker wasn't locked, which I'd both hoped for and sort of expected. I never saw her carrying any keys around or locking any doors. It was the middle of nowhere, and it seemed to me that security was pretty well covered by the looming fact of her awfulness. No one, and I mean *no one*, wanted to be on Mrs. Goring's bad side. I could think of little else that would upset her more than someone breaking into her house.

Davis didn't stay in the fort for more than ten minutes before he was back out again. I'd only just gotten up the courage to run across the clearing, open Mrs. Goring's door, and slip inside. I caught sight of him coming out as I was going in and wondered if he'd guessed where I was.

I made my way downstairs, finding the door to the basement open as well, alert for Mrs. Goring's return from delivering lunch. Davis was in the woods, either searching for me or heading up the path for home, so at least I was safe for the moment.

Pulling the bomb shelter door nearly closed, I settled in and switched the monitor back on. They were at the table, eating and talking, as I tried to catch a glimpse of Ben Dugan's T-shirt but couldn't. A badge of honor, I supposed, some kind of camp T-shirt you got if you let them scare you half to death.

Soon enough Mrs. Goring was back, the door into the basement pulled shut, and I was sealed in once more. I lay on the cot, so tired, and my young brother haunted my half-wakeful dreams.

That Davis dude is trouble. He can have whatever girl he wants. Better get with it.

What do you know? You're like ten

I'm thirteen, Will. And I've had a lot more dates than you. Trust me.

Shut up, Keith. You're an idiot.

Maybe I'll give Marisa a try. She's not half bad, especially that T-shirt. What a come-on.

I'm going to hit you now.

I dare you.

The dream dissolved into madness, my fist hitting Keith's face and the two of us tumbling down a flight of winding stairs into darkness, our limbs hopelessly entangled. When we hit the bottom, Keith was gone;

but Dr. Stevens was there, standing in the blue room, holding the helmet.

Sit down. I have something for you.

I won't.

Are you sure?

I woke in a sweat, looked at my watch, and groaned. 3:13 PM. Such a vivid dream, almost real. I shook my head awake and tried to calm down. The monitor was lifeless, and I thought with some alarm that the system had died again. I didn't remember turning it off, but I must have, because when I clicked the M button, the main room was there again. I saw the black opening to the stairs and trembled. Everyone was seated at the table, including Rainsford, his back facing the camera. When was I going to see this guy's face, I thought, and it was as if he'd heard me speak.

He got up, appeared to be talking, then turned in my direction, walking slowly with his hands behind his back.

"Wow, he's old," I said. It was the very first thing that came into my mind. Rainsford looked ancient. He walked with a slow gait, as if his knees were failing him. Silver hair, thick eyebrows, a thin face. If he and Mrs. Goring were in a cage match, he'd get his butt handed to him.

It was frustrating not being able to hear his voice. He didn't look directly into the camera, more to the side; but even seeing him made me want to give up the fight. The way he moved when he spoke was almost hypnotic, a certain cadence that dulled the senses.

He turned, and Kate Hollander got up.

I could almost hear her saying the words as she came alongside him.

"I'm ready."

The two walked together until they reached the door to the girls' quarters. He touched her gently on the shoulder and she went inside. No one at the table moved as Rainsford slowly walked past and started down the winding stairs, back to his private chambers. I couldn't help thinking he'd break his neck on the way down. After Rainsford was gone I felt a tingling in my foot and realized it had fallen asleep. The rest of me seemed to have already awoken from a dream.

What just happened? Did I see him or dream him? It was hard to tell if I'd awoken from a dream within a dream.

I pressed the white G-for-girls button, and the screen popped to life with an empty chair and three numbers stenciled in red on the back wall.

2, 5, 7

I put in my earbuds as Kate entered the room and sat down to face Dr. Stevens's monitor. I dialed up one of Kate's sessions with Dr. Stevens. Watching her was so strange, the words in my head not quite matching up; and yet somehow it all felt orchestrated.

What if you're really sick; have you thought of that?

That's just stupid. Look at me. I'm fine.

Looks can be deceiving.

Not in my case. What you see is what you get.

You know, Kate, the doctors won't hurt you.

Tell that to my mom.

They're not hurting her. They're trying to help.

Nineteen surgeries and her head is still a mess. Sounds like a failure from where I'm sitting.

Let's talk about that, about where you were when the accident happened.

Let's not.

It's important, Kate.

No, it's not. And I don't want to talk about it.

That was how it went with Kate Hollander. She was terrified of doctors, of anyone who might try to fix her. There were times in those sessions when it sounded as if Kate was in charge and Dr. Stevens was not. But through scores of audio files I had also discovered a many-faceted Kate. She could be calm, lucid. Sometimes she would cry because of her fear or because of a terrible guilt. And in those times she was tender, like a small child. At her most vulnerable, she would say things I didn't understand.

I like the pain. It's mine; I can control it.

And in those times I began to understand that her fear wasn't really about doctors but about something deeper, something I didn't fully understand. I knew her mother had been in an accident and that the accident had scarred her head and face, robbed her of her beauty and something more. Kate's mom was never the same after. She was not missing but was not altogether there anymore, either.

Kate Hollander got up, and I took out my earbuds. She had a thick paintbrush in her hand, as Ben Dugan had; and walking to the wall, she obliterated the number 2 in a crush of purple paint. When she was done, she dropped the brush at her feet without turning around, rubbed the back of her head like it might be bothering her, and left the room.

I wondered again what it meant to destroy the numbers, but I was starting to catch on. If Kate was number 2, than she was wiping out her fear, and with it, some part of herself.

I cycled quickly to the main floor and caught her coming out of the girls' quarters, looking back at the table where everyone was waiting for her. Connor made a sort of fist-charging sign, and others were rooting her on. She turned to that middle door, the one between the boys' and the girls' rooms, and opened it.

She was gone, and I started to think about where on earth she was going. I'd thought it all through, mapping everything out like a level on a video game screen. There had to be a long hall and at the end, stairs.

How far down was the room Kate would enter, where she would find the strange helmet dangling from wires? If it was at the same level as Rainsford's quarters, it was far down into the depths of the earth.

A long time, what felt like an hour, passed in the bomb shelter. No one seemed to move in the main room. Stillness had invaded the world of Eden.

The screen on one of the six dead monitors began to flutter. There was the monitor in the very middle—the one I could control—and six that went around it in a perfect circle. Ben had been on top, and now Kate would fill the first monitor to the right; that would be hers.

I was struck by the room itself, which was different from Ben Dugan's in two ways. First, it was not blue, but deep purple, coarsely painted and shot through with streaks of black. Second, Ben Dugan had found a simple wooden chair; but Kate's chair was more elaborate, a barber's chair or something like it.

What was the same about the room could not be missed: the helmet was there, sitting on the barber's chair, its torrent of wires and tubes rising into the ceiling.

By my watch, which I had used to time the event, it took Kate Hollander only three minutes to get from the main room in Fort Eden to the purple room with the barber's chair. *Three minutes?* It had seemed so much longer. It ruled out a long flight of treacherous stairs, so there must have been some other way down into the deep.

As with Ben's video feed, I was getting some strange sounds from somewhere inside the wall: deep electrical static I'd never heard before entering the bomb shelter.

Kate picked up the helmet, put it on, and sat in the barber's chair. The screen filled with data as it had done before. The mercury line on the right of the screen, a bobbing dot of purple waiting to lift off, and in the top left corner, words:

Kate Hollander, 15
Acute fear: Doctors, hospitals, clinics

For a long beat nothing happened, and I began to wonder if Kate Hollander's resolve was stronger than the cure Rainsford had devised. Then the chair started spinning around, first to one side and then to the other, like it was controlled by an unseen hand.

Sorry, Kate, I thought. *I think the trouble's just begun.*

What was on the screen melted away, replaced by a doctor in a white coat. I was seeing inside the helmet, the same scene Kate saw; and I wondered again where the images came from. The doctor was suddenly up close, a spot of blood the size of a dime on the corner of his white mask. He looked at me, which meant he was looking at Kate, tilting his head to and fro like a creature planning its attack. The eyes were all wrong, at once vacant and searching. His hand came up close to the screen, and he snapped on a plastic glove. Was he speaking to her? With the mask, I couldn't tell.

The image spun wildly, and the screen jerked back to the purple room, where the barber's chair spun, too. Kate Hollander was holding on with white-knuckled fingers.

The screen jumped back to what Kate saw: the back of a woman's head, full of blond hair. She was driving a car, so the view was from someone in the backseat.

The camera angle sloshed downward, revealing small legs tucked into a car seat. A child of five or six, and the child's stuffed animal had fallen to the backseat floor. All the while, strange sounds filled the bomb shelter, as if the wall of monitors was digging its way out of a hopeless dream.

There's more sound this time than last, I thought. *And the sounds are worse.*

The chair spun again, the screen switching back and forth from the purple room to the insanity inside the helmet. The doctor was facing away, but when he turned, he held a rusted metal contraption that was clearly designed to fit over a patient's head. There were long bolts aimed into the center, decayed with age and sharp at the ends. He advanced, placed whatever this thing was on Kate's head, and began spinning the bolts. I found myself wincing for poor Kate Hollander.

The screen went wild again, landing in the car, where the woman at the wheel had turned to the child as they drove. They were talking, the child agitated about the lost toy on the floor and trying to free herself from the car seat. The woman—Kate's mother, it had to be—was looking back and forth between the road and the child, her arm reaching blindly for the backseat floor.

The chair spun again, found the doctor moving in, squirting a line of purple liquid from a long needle.

Oh no. This is bad, I thought, the screen veered wildly, focusing on Kate gripping the barber's chair, but only held the image for a second before the doctor reappeared.[2]

There was a central question above all the others as the doctor wielded a hacksaw, sharpening it against a stone in his hand: *Why are you doing this to us?* It looked as if the doctor was planning to use the saw on Kate's head; but as he moved closer, the chair spun again. The purple line on the edge of the screen was moving fast, faster than it had for Ben Dugan. Kate Hollander was terrified.

A weird sound from the wall—like a boat engine echoing up and down on a choppy sea—and the screen

---

[2] *How does he know these things about us?* I asked myself.
I was prepared to answer in one of three ways:

1) Rainsford had been following each of us for a long time, recording these events or, worse, setting them in motion.

2) The helmet had opened Kate's and Ben's minds. Rainsford had devised a way to find a certain kind of memory, then bring it to life inside the helmet and on the screens I watched.

3) Dr. Stevens had revealed every last detail of every last fear, somehow gathering the information from relatives or hypnosis sessions or who knew how, and the scenes had been meticulously re-created in order to evoke a feeling of extreme fear.

returned to the car, where Kate's mom was leaning down over the seat, staring at the floor, the road wobbly behind her.

Then the semitruck.

And after that a burst of hard, white light paired with a brutal noise I never want to hear again: an awful churning sound, like big rocks tumbling inside a cement mixer.

The monitor flashed back to Kate, where the purple line had reached the top of the screen. The wires in the room shot to life. Kate shook violently, but only for a moment, and then it was done.

The purple room went soft and quiet as the chair spun slightly to one side, like a tricycle bumping into a curb on a dead end street. The only sound in the bomb shelter was my own breathing.

She wasn't moving, but I'd seen this once before and knew she wasn't dead. Far from it. As the image of the purple room crackled on the monitor and then vanished entirely, I understood what had happened.

Kate Hollander had been cured.

CONNOR AND ALEX

I didn't worry as much about Kate as I had Ben, and I expected to worry even less about Connor. In that way, the cures were like a video game. I played mostly old games—Berzerk, Donkey Kong, stuff like that—but once in a while I'd wander into Keith's room. He had an Xbox, but I called it his Death-box. If I hadn't been in there for a while, say a couple of weeks, I'd find myself stunned by the blood and the guns, the ridiculous body count in the games he plays. Funny thing, though. If

I hung around for a few minutes, it started to bother me less. A half hour later, if I was still in the room, I wouldn't care anymore. The blood and the bodies were meaningless.

When I saw Ben Dugan get cured, I felt real pain, as if a person had been snuffed out of existence. And I was afraid. If Ben was dead, I could be next, and I wasn't ready to be dead. Plus, whatever he'd gone through had looked painful and electrifying in its terror.

With Kate, I knew the truth. She'd been scared, but not literally to death. Knowing this took the sting out of the proceedings and, frankly, not in a good way. I was turning numb to it all. This feeling would deepen, I knew, with Connor and Alex. But what would happen when Marisa put the helmet on? That one I would feel.

Maybe I'd even get back what the cures were taking from me.

Something very important happened while I was waiting for the central monitor to kick back on again. It happened because I was in a state of extreme boredom.

I'd finished reading *The Pearl*, a short book I was keen

to talk about with Marisa, and had begun *The Woman in the Dunes*. But I wasn't a big reader, and I'd already read quite a lot. With nothing else to do, I ate a Clif Bar and dumped out the entire contents of my backpack. I emptied every single zipper compartment, for no other reason than it was something to do besides stare at the walls. Inside one of the small pouches I found a crappy little MP3 player I hadn't packed, which I recognized immediately as Keith's. The thing was tiny and ancient, the only kind my penniless brother could afford. It wasn't even made by Apple. He'd stuck a yellow Post-it Note to the player, but it had fallen off and lay in the bottom of the pouch. I picked it up and stuck it to my finger.

I am playing Berzerk. Get well. Keith.

He was a huge punk, but for some reason, the note made me choke up inside, my throat tightening as it had in the van on the way to Fort Eden. I missed his competitive goofiness. And it was kind of a big deal, him sending the player. He was always walking around the house with earbuds in, listening to classic rock and roll, which he claimed made him smarter. By sending the note and the player, he was trying to help me in his small way, even if he'd never admit it. Going without his music would be a sacrifice. He'd have to listen to my mom nag him all day.

The white earbuds he'd sent along were caked with earwax, so I stuffed them back in the side pouch of my backpack and got my own. Mine were black and perfectly clean. If I wore them under my hoodie, it was hard to tell I had them on at all, which I liked very much. I pulled up the hood and cranked up the volume.

I did not recognize the first song or the second, but the third was Kiss—"Detroit Rock City"—which told the tale of someone hitting a semitruck head-on. Coincidence? I don't know, but it connected me to Kate and the others in an unexpected way. I clicked back and played it again, listening for words I'd missed, and walked out into the basement. It was dark out there, but a shaft of light from the bomb shelter poured into the shadows as I started aimlessly looking at cans and boxes. I let one earbud dangle at my side and listened through a single ear, just in case Mrs. Goring arrived unexpectedly. Around the corner where the electrical panel was, it was too dark to see, so I turned on the basement light. When I went back, the song was over and I started it again. A mindless tune, really, but it was growing on me. I could see why Keith liked the way it blocked out the rest of the world.

There was a set of metal shelves next to the electrical panel I'd only glanced at before. A tarp, caked with dirt, was stuffed into the bottom shelf like a giant wadded-up Kleenex. The second shelf was covered with old paint cans and mason jars filled with nails, screws, washers. The top shelf was harder to see, its surface above my sight line, but it looked like more of the same: some old coffee cans filled with things I didn't care to look at, an oil pan, a lunch pail.

The lunch pail caught my attention, and I felt surprised I hadn't noticed it sooner. It was the big green kind a carpenter takes to a work site, rectangular at the bottom and curved on top. When I was a kid, I'd imagined myself with hammers and saws, building a house, carrying my lunch in just such an object. I reached up and lifted it by the handle.

"Whoa, this thing's heavy," I said, setting it on the concrete floor with a weighty *thunk.* I picked it back up and looked at the bottom, where someone had used a thick black pen to write the word GORING in all caps. "Detroit Rock City" was coming to an end in my one earbud as I set the box back down, the car going ninety-five in the song, swerving in front of the oncoming semi. I popped the two rusty latches on the lunch pail and tipped open the top. Inside, wadded up in a tangled mess, was the one thing I'd wanted more than anything else.

Headphones.

Not earbuds but *real* headphones, big ones that would stick out on the sides of my head like giant monkey ears. I took them out, letting the glob of twirling cord flop out of the box.

A Who song, "My Generation," started playing in my ear, and I pulled out the earbud. Holding the end of the headphone cord in my hand, I examined three strange plugs, as wide as if they'd fit into a car cigarette lighter—their size a perfect match to the holes in the wall of monitors. I was fast on my feet, my shoes sliding as I rounded the corner. When I reached the bomb shelter, I untangled the long, thick coil that led from the headphones to the connectors.

"Come on, work. Give me something I can use," I said, placing the headphones over my ears. They were so old that the plastic on the wide ear coverings was cracked and brittle. And they were big, so big my hoodie wouldn't fit over the top without stretching. Not the most comfortable pair of headphones I'd ever worn, but they were one of a kind. They were made for the bomb shelter monitors, and this I knew, because the three connectors snapped into the holes in the wall with ease.

I was plugged in.

Now all I needed was a system that actually worked.

I stood at the wall of monitors, cycling through all four buttons, but there was almost nothing. A slight humming noise, like electricity running through power lines overhead, buzzed in my ears.

I looked at my watch, 11:04 PM. If Marisa was trying to send me a message, I couldn't see it. I set the headphones on the cot and went into the basement, where I turned off the light and put the green lunch pail back where I'd found it. When I returned, I dialed down the light in the bomb shelter and pushed the white G-for-girls button. I put the headphones back on and sat down on the rickety cot, waiting.

Ten minutes later I fell asleep.

Kate's head hurts.

She hasn't come back to see me. How's she doing otherwise?

Great. She went to bed early, like 10:30. She was tired, but different.

Different how?

She's not afraid anymore.

How do you know for sure?

I know what it looks like in a girl. She's cured.

My eyes came open and I moved, but I couldn't hear the squeaky springs on the cot. My ears felt smashed and hot, and there were voices.

That's very good news, Marisa. Are you excited? It won't be long now.

I guess I am. It's so mysterious, you know? Kate says she can't remember what happened; she just woke up and knew.

It will be the same for you.

I was drawn rapidly out of sleep and stood before the wall of monitors.

"I can hear you," I said, barely hearing my own voice through thick foam and cracked plastic. "I can hear what you're saying."

"So anyway, I just wanted to say *everyone* went to

sleep. You know me, always the last one."

Marisa glanced at the floor and then back at the screen as if she was looking at me, not Dr. Stevens.

"Just a little longer. Hang in there, okay?"

"Okay. Sorry to call so late."

"It's never a problem, Marisa. Anytime."

Marisa got up out of the chair, and I heard the door open and close.

"I gotta move, and fast," I said, jamming the stuff in my backpack that I'd poured out on the floor. It was amazing how fast I'd turned the bomb shelter into something that looked more like my room back home. I hadn't just dumped out my pack, I'd stacked things in piles. Extra clothes, my Recorder and Keith's MP3 player, a mountain of Clif Bars, bottles of water all in a row. I'd stacked it all neatly against the wall while emptying my bag, then neglected to put it all back once I had on the super-sized headphones. I took less care putting my things away, stuffing the shirts and then the bars and the bottles like a marine packing to get out of a foxhole under fire. The headphones were still on, that slight sound of static dancing in my ears; and then voices appeared, crisp and unexpected, and I turned to the wall of monitors. The room was still empty, but Dr.

Stevens was speaking to someone who had a gravelly old voice. Rainsford. Had to be.

She's not ready yet. Better finish off the boys first.

I can take them both at once. It's what they want. I've seen to it.

We're not even halfway there. Don't overdo it. And we still haven't found Will Besting.

Davis will find him. I have little doubt of that.

There was a static-filled pause, the click of a button, and then more.

I'm not sure she can be trusted.

Don't be ridiculous. Of course she can. She'll play her part; I'll see to it.

Fine.

[Off channel marker. 12:21 AM.]

I took off the headphones and pulled the plugs from the wall, my ears adjusting to dead silence.

I'm not sure she can be trusted.

I didn't want to know what that meant, but there it was: one of us wasn't who they appeared to be. Someone was in on whatever was happening, a *she*. Kate Hollander or Avery Varone, I told myself. It's one of them. They're keeping an eye on everyone, making sure no one steps out of line. One of them is a mole.

I walked into the basement and put the headphones back into the lunch pail, returning it to the top shelf, and then finished packing my things away. I was tired of carrying my backpack around and hid it on one of the shelves in the basement. One back pocket filled with my Recorder, the other with my paperback copy of *The Pearl*, and I was ready to go.

All the while, a single thought ran through my head, over and over, until I was up the ramp and pushing the door open into Fort Eden.

Please don't let it be Marisa.

She sat closer to me on the couch from the start, and she looked at me as if she'd missed me. Thoughts of betrayal were already melting away, but I was cautious, a little guarded.

"I hope Rainsford doesn't come out here and catch us. Or Mrs. Goring. That would be bad."

She told me they wouldn't, brushing over it as if it didn't really matter, and I began to worry that the whole thing was a setup. Everyone would arrive, all at once, and I'd be trapped. Mrs. Goring from the basement, Rainsford from the winding stone stairs, the other kids from the back rooms; they'd crawl out from every corner of the fort like rats and corner me.

"Don't be nervous, Will," Marisa said. She knew me already. She could tell I was struggling. "No one is going to find us."

She reached out and touched my hand, her fingers soft and trembling in the dark, and my heart skipped a beat.

"You haven't told anyone about where I'm hiding?" I asked.

"No, I haven't," she answered, the slightest wisp of defensiveness in her voice, the hand pulled away. "You'll come back when you're ready. You just need time."

"What if I don't?"

"Then you don't. But I think you should."

"Why?"

"Because, Will. It works. Kate's cured."

"How can you tell for sure? There are no doctors out here in the woods."

Marisa's dark brow furrowed, and her head tilted. How had I known what Kate was afraid of? I'd slipped, but she let it pass.

"You know what it means to be afraid," she went on. "You know what it looks like. There's a certain something, always there no matter what. Both Kate and Ben had it, like you and me. But it's gone now."

She looked at me, and I felt the wall I'd put up between us start to crumble and fall. If she was going to tell them where I was, she would have done it already.

"I have to tell you something."

There were many reasons why I told her that night in Fort Eden: the crushing guilt, the loneliness, the absolute fear of being caught and thrown into a room at the bottom of the world. But mostly, I just wanted to hold her hand one more time. After that I could die in peace. Maybe my best and only hope was to come clean.

And so I told her many things, but not all. I told her about the audio files, making sure to mention the part about how I truly felt I *had* to take them. I told her I'd discovered headphones that would let me hear, but that I absolutely would not break our trust and listen when

I felt I shouldn't. I told her it was lonely in the bomb shelter and that I didn't trust anyone but her. I stopped short of telling about the colored rooms and what went on inside them, because I still wasn't sure if I should rob her of a chance to be cured, no matter how bizarre the methods were. If she knew, she'd never go through with it.

After that, the hardest part of all.

I told her what I feared.

"I'm afraid of people," I said; "it's why I couldn't come in here." And just as quickly, she answered, "I know. It's okay."

Was it that obvious? The trembling hand was back, and I breathed deeply for a moment that I wished would never end.

"I can be at home," I went on, encouraged. "My younger brother is irritating, but I can be around him. And my parents and Dr. Stevens, but that's about it."

"And me," she added, and I realized she was right.

"Yeah, and you."

She took her hand away once more and rubbed her palms on her flannel pajamas.

"So I don't need to tell you what I'm afraid of, you already know?"

"I do, and I'm sorry."

It was a big sorry, full with meaning, and she understood: I was sorry for my mistake; but much more, I was sorry she had to be afraid. I had imagined what this moment would be like. She'd get up and leave and never come back or run through the fort knocking on doors, telling everyone what I'd done.

She didn't say anything at all though, and she didn't move. She just stared at her shoes as if she was thinking of standing on them and walking away but couldn't quite make herself do it. Her head tilted up, staring out into space.

"It's nice not having to tell. I don't like talking about it. But what you did was wrong."

"I know it was."

More silence, and I was sure what had begun between us had already found its end. Then her voice.

"I might have done the same thing if I'd thought I could get away with it."

I needed a perfect answer, and for once I think I got it right.

"No, you wouldn't have. You're better than that."

She looked away, hiding a fleeting smile, and delivered the verdict.

"No more hand holding for twenty-four hours."

A fitting punishment, because it was the only thing I wanted.

We never got around to taking the books out and talking about them. Our conversation drifted into what we'd been doing while we were apart. I told her about seeing Davis; she told me that Avery was falling hard for him. She told me that Kate was having headaches, and Ben was still feeling a little sore in his joints—aftereffects of the treatments, which Rainsford assured them would soon pass.

I asked why no one went near the winding staircase that led down to Rainsford's room; she said he had told them not to, so they didn't. I asked about the door between the rooms where people went to be cured; she said it was for a certain purpose. No one went through there until it was their time.

There was that part of her that seemed too compliant—a part I didn't understand—as if someone else controlled a piece but not all of her mind. It was this part of her that made me come back an hour later, after she was finally asleep.

It was time for me to open the middle door and see what was behind it.

Don't be nervous, Will. No one is going to find us.

Marisa's greeting from earlier in the night repeated in my head, the kind of thing a girl might say if she was inviting you into her bedroom for the first time. At least that's what I imagined as I stared down the hallway. Why couldn't we be in her room instead of discovering each other in a madhouse?

I'd opened the heavy door, which on closer inspection was solid oak. It was the kind of weighty slab of wood I feared getting my fingers caught in, a real bone breaker; and as far as I could tell, it had no lock.

Behind the door, a few feet back, a heavy black curtain.

I pulled the door closed behind me and felt a bottomless twist in my gut, like I'd sealed myself in a coffin and a gravedigger was about to start throwing dirt on top of me. I parted the curtain at the middle and stepped through, and saw a faint light overhead at the end of a long hallway. The hall reminded me of the ramp up out of the basement between the Bunker and Fort Eden, only it was shorter and tilting downward. There was a rail on either side, and on the sloping floor before me, grave black-and-white images. Looking down, I found that I was standing on a painting of Kino, the man from the book who'd found the pearl. He was floating down the floor in a canoe, his back to me. Farther away, there he was again, smaller in the distance, and again smaller still under a pale bulb of light at the end of the hall. The way down had the appearance of a man floating away from something, or *into* something; it was hard to say what the meaning was.

I held one of the rails and started walking, but stopped short at the sound of a distant whispering voice radiating from the deep. It sounded like someone was searching down the long hallways of my mind, trying to find me but failing. I snapped a picture of the floor with my Recorder, then put in my earbuds and played the sounds from the pond in my ears: splashing water, voices, birds, and wind in the trees. The whispering fell away in the forest and I walked, pulling up my dark hood. The ramp leveled out at the bottom, where a black-and-white image of Kino painted on one side of an elevator door stood staring at me. In one hand he held the pearl, dripping with water or blood, I couldn't say which. In his other hand he held the standing canoe, the top of which was cut off by the top of the elevator. To the right of the elevator door, a glowing orange button with a down arrow.

Am I really doing this? I asked myself, my finger hovering over the gleaming round button. *What if the door opens and it's a shaft a hundred feet deep? I could fall in. What if Rainsford is standing inside and I'm caught? What if he grabs me and pulls me into a room and shoves a helmet on my head? Then what?*

I tapped my Recorder off and found that the whispering had stopped. Dead silence as the painting of Kino, a big man with a face like stone, stared at me. His face did not say one thing or another, not *Follow me* or *Turn back, you fool*. It was a vacant stare, like the decision had already been made and could not be unmade. I willed myself to push the button. When the doors opened, I saw a small square window dead center against the back wall, a black zero painted on the stone behind it. I leaned my head inside a wood-paneled elevator and was relieved to find both an UP and a DOWN button.

At least it goes both ways. If I go down, I should be able to come back up again.

I stepped inside; and as the doors began to move in from both sides, the whispering started again. This time I had a harder time telling my thumb to touch the button of my Recorder, filling my head with sounds. The voice was hypnotic. It was digging, trying to get inside.

I spun the dial to a song I'd downloaded weeks ago and had heard a hundred times already: *I wanna be adored*, which I fast-forwarded into deafening guitar and vocals.

When I looked up, the doors to the elevator had closed and I was moving. I pushed the UP button over and over, but it had no effect. I was going down to the very bottom whether I liked it or not.

The inside of the elevator doors were painted, too, but Kino was gone. His canoe lay smashed against the rocks, broken into pieces. As the elevator moved down into the depths of Fort Eden, I wondered how deep I was going. Fifty feet, a hundred? The song played through and I started it again before the ride was over and the doors slowly began to open. I held them open but didn't leave the safety of the elevator; outside the floor slanted downward, going deeper still. Kino and his canoe were gone, replaced by a floor of dirt and stone. It smelled of cold earth, a smell of being buried alive.

The door didn't act as an elevator door should, pushing against my hand every few seconds like a mouth trying to shut. I took my hand away and the doors held, waiting, it seemed, until someone pushed the UP button.

"These are the rooms," I whispered, though I couldn't

hear my own voice over the music. Outside my head, beyond the noise, the whispering voice would draw me deeper still, until the helmet was on my head and I was screaming.

No thanks, I think I'll pass.

I risked a foot against a flat stone outside, then another; and without really thinking about it, I found that I'd stepped out of the elevator and into the realm of rooms.

"Ben's," I said, turning to my right first and then my left. "And Kate's."

I kept the music playing but snapped pictures as well: the walls, the doors. On Ben's side a mural of bugs, like gothic graffiti or a paisley tie gone completely insane, and on Kate's the same style of artistry, only swirling scalpels and drills and saws. I looked inside Ben's blue room, where soft light bathed the chair in which he'd sat. Leaning inside the other room, I saw purple walls and the barber's chair. The floor was flat in the rooms, unlike the one in the deeply sloping stone hall I stood in, which made the whole place feel like a crooked house at a badly run-down theme park. There was no sign of a wired helmet in either room; it was like I'd dreamed the helmets' existence from the start.

On each of the doors, a square and a number, stenciled like I'd seen in the rooms with Dr. Stevens's monitor.

Ben's door: number 1.

Kate's door: number 2.

Beyond the two rooms, at the end of a short hall, was another thick black curtain. I pushed it aside gently and peeked through. Two more rooms, two more walls, and yet another curtain at the far end. I knew by what was painted on the walls that the rooms were for Connor and Alex. I snapped pictures of the mysterious paintings and the doors marked with a 3 and a 4.

I didn't need to go any farther, as the entire basement mapped itself out in my mind: there would be six rooms, three on each side of the hall, separated in pairs by dark curtains leading down, down, down. But I kept going anyway, drawn into the farthest depths of Fort Eden by an unseen, malevolent force.

Through the last hallway curtain I found a wall on my right covered with a painting of giant, swirling mushrooms and a locked door stenciled with a number 5. It had to be Marisa's room, but the image made no sense at all. The thought of her sitting in there with that helmet on made me angry, but it also made me wonder: could whatever happened in there actually cure Marisa? As twisted as this place was, was it my obligation to take that from her? Nothing I knew of Marisa led me to believe that mushrooms had anything to do with what she was afraid of. It was a mystery that threatened to draw me closer in, until I glanced across at the other side of the hallway and saw a door with the number 6 on it. The wall was utterly blank, which stood to reason. I had been ignored or forgotten. I wasn't there. I was alone. There wasn't anything they could paint on my wall, because no one knew me.

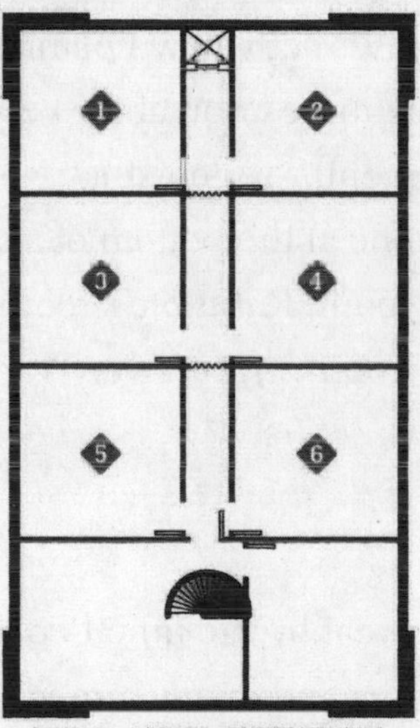

FORT EDEN BASEMENT

Must feel nice, being invisible. No chores, I imagined Keith saying at the doorjamb of room number 6. For some reason, in my mind's eye, a bead of blood was trickling down his nose.

Come on, you'll love it in here. They got Death-boxes galore.

Go home, Keith! I don't want you here.

I shook the cobwebs from my head and dialed up the volume on the song.

Staring at the door, I knew the truth: room number 6 was my room. Probably it would be empty on the other side, too, which is exactly how I planned to keep it.

There was one more door, at the very end of the long hallway. The seventh, a door that would open into a room that sat alone at the bottom of a spiral staircase.

The seventh room, *Rainsford*'s room.

And the only room left for Avery Varone.

I was in a cold sweat by the time I collapsed on the cot in the bomb shelter and finally turned off the music. My hands were shaking, and my breath came in deep waves as if, like Kino, I had been underwater for a long, long time searching for something of great value. It had been, I decided, the most terrifying night of my life. Something about not being able to hear the world around me amplified the terror ten times. I couldn't hear someone coming after me as I made my night journey back to the Bunker, and that, more than anything else, had almost crippled me with fear.

Looking at my watch for the first time in more than an hour, I was surprised to see just how late it was: 3:40 AM. A few more hours and the sun would be up. Mrs. Goring would return with her stupid banging food cart, and I'd be scared all over again. I didn't know how much more I could take, and vowed right then in the bomb shelter to get away. I'd find some way to tell Marisa—a note or a whisper when no one was around—and we'd run. We'd run up the path until we found Davis's car parked on the washboard road. I didn't have a license and neither did she, but we'd crash right through the gate, out of the wilderness, and get back to our normal lives.

Mrs. Goring's not going to come in here, I told myself. I was so tired I couldn't keep my eyes open. I hadn't even turned on the light in the bomb shelter. I'd just pulled the door almost closed and fallen dead asleep on the cot, staring at the black ceiling.

Gotta set the alarm on my watch. Gotta do that. Gotta do it right now.

But I didn't.

The thing about a bomb shelter tucked away in the corner of an entombed cement basement is this: it's stunningly quiet. I could only guess that Mrs. Goring, for some unknown reason, had neglected to feed the guests. Or maybe she'd gone the other way around and delivered a box of cold cereal and a gallon of milk, an errand that wouldn't require a rolling cart. Either way, I'd slept for a very, very long time. So long, in fact, that, looking at my watch, I was unsure if it was night or day in the world outside.

4:15. I thought I'd only slept for a half hour, but then I blinked fully awake and saw the tiny letters: PM.

"Oh no," I tried to say, but the words were more of a thought as they crept past my dusty throat. I reached for a bottle of water and guzzled six or seven gulps, feeling the empty space in my belly.

Hungry didn't begin to cover how famished I was, but the idea of one more Clif Bar was so depressing, I couldn't bring myself to rip one out of its package.

"I need food. *Real* food."

My mind wandered to Kino in his canoe as I riffled through boxes and cans on the shelves in the basement. I could see him paddling out to sea, leaving everything behind. It was a peaceful thought, until the canoe was smashed into a thousand pieces in my mind, as it had been in the story. It seemed that for Kino, the pearl invited nothing but misfortune.

Mrs. Goring had done some canning, or someone had, and I searched through a shelf filled with jars of peaches and pickles.

"No way she'll notice just one," I said, taking a jar of the golden peaches and heading for the electrical panel. There I grabbed the metal lunch pail in my other hand and returned to the bomb shelter. About a minute later I was standing in front of the main monitor, the giant headphones on, digging sliced peaches out of the jar.

Everyone was in the main room, even Mrs. Goring, and Davis had returned.

"Thanks for the chicken," Connor was saying, licking his fingers. "Just what the doctor ordered."

"I've eaten Mrs. Goring's dinners," Davis said, playfully it seemed, but also a bit cutting. "Good to get a break."

A KFC bucket rested on the round table, where all the guys sat eating greasy chicken.

"Nobody starves around here," Mrs. Goring commented. "You of all people should know that."

I couldn't see Marisa, which bothered me. Maybe she was outside, or sleeping in the girls' quarters where I couldn't see. Cycling through the monitors yielded no sign of her, and I worried as Davis went on.

"I think I'll stay and sleep in the guys' room tonight; there's an extra bed in there."

"Suit yourself," Mrs. Goring said. "Just stay out of my way and don't make a mess. You know the drill."

"Yes, ma'am."

"No luck yet with Will?" asked Avery. She was sitting on the couch close to Davis.

"I'm heading out again as soon as these guys get going. He has to be getting tired of sleeping out there. It got pretty cold last night."

"Let's do this thing," Connor said, wiping the back of his hand across his face. Years of heroics on the field were likely to help Connor endure whatever Rainsford threw at him. "I'm ready to get it over with."

"Me, too," said Alex, although a lot less forcefully. Scoring high on the style chart wasn't likely to offer much in the way of comfort during a cure.

"You're positive you guys want to go at the same time?"

asked Ben Dugan. "I'm not even sure that's possible."

"It's fine, right, Mrs. Goring?" asked Davis. He'd sat down next to Avery, the two of them practically touching shoulders.

"Whatever Rainsford says. How should I know?"

"Maybe it's better to wait until we find out for sure," Avery said.

"You just don't want it to be your turn; that's what this is really about," Kate said. She'd clearly given up the battle for Davis's affection and wanted to get a dig in at Avery.

"I already told you," Avery replied flatly. "I'm not going. I can't be cured."

There it was again, that Avery Varone defiance, as if her fear was worse than anyone else's. A big part of me wanted to cede Kate the point. Knowing what I knew, it was hard to imagine a worse situation than what Kate had lived with.

"I think Avery's right," said Davis, surprising no one. He and Avery were rapidly growing closer to each other. "It's early yet, and besides, he'll want to talk to you before you guys go."

He looked at Avery and said something I could barely hear. "But you're wrong. You can be cured. You just have to believe."

"No, I can't," Avery replied, a wistful smile on her face, as if it didn't matter either way as long as Davis was around.

Kate appeared to roll her eyes, but she was pretty far away from the camera, so I couldn't say for sure. She was wearing a T-shirt like Ben's, white with some sort of emblem on the front—the letter *E*.

"What the heck is that thing?" I said out loud, dripping peach juice down my chin and wiping it away with the sleeve of my hoodie. The peaches were sweet and gooey, and it tasted like Mrs. Goring had thrown cinnamon in there, too.

Davis touched Avery on the hand and told everyone he was heading out to look for me until Rainsford came back, which made me nervous. It was only a matter of time before he'd start to wonder, *Could that kid have actually gone inside Mrs. Goring's bunker?*

I took off the headphones and went back into the basement so I could find a place to hide a half-empty jar of peaches. I ended up stuffing the remains behind the tarp by the electrical panel, where I was sure Mrs. Goring would never find them. I was still hungry, and looking along the food shelves, I found a row of boxed crackers. A box of saltines was already open, and I slid a long, wrapped package of them out.

Two people had appeared while I was gone; and taking them together, they added up to one very bad thing. Marisa and Rainsford were both standing in the main room in front of the door to the girls' quarters.

"They were together," I said, and I imagined I was still holding the glass jar as it slipped through my fingers and smashed all over the floor. I threw the package of crackers on the cot and put the headphones back on, hoping for some clue to where they'd been and what they'd talked about. I couldn't verify that Marisa had told my secret, and neither could I be sure that Rainsford knew anything at all about my whereabouts; but doubt had seeped into the bomb shelter. *What had they spoken about if not me?*

"Maybe he took the elevator," I said, wanting to give Marisa the benefit of the doubt.

"Davis?"

It was a word I'd heard Rainsford say many times: *Davis*. It was as if he felt Davis's absence the second he arrived in the room. It was a question: *Davis, where are you?* But there was also confusion in his voice: *Where has Davis gone in my absence?* And one more thing, deeper still in the voice: an accusation. *I told him to stay here. He should not have wandered off.*

"He's looking for Will Besting," said Avery, pointing to the main entryway. "Out there."

"Of course he is," Rainsford agreed, smiling as if he'd simply let the fact slip from his mind but had remembered now. He moved on to more pressing matters.

"Kate, how are the headaches? he asked. "Better, I hope." They were all standing in a circle around him like they were five and he was about to hand out bags of candy.

"Yeah, I feel much better. Totally better," Kate said, but it was so obviously a lie that Mrs. Goring caught on.

"In a pig's eye," she said. "Stay put. I'll get you another aspirin."

Rainsford seemed more willing to believe Kate's answer and didn't acknowledge Mrs. Goring other than to nod appreciatively.

"Ben, you've recovered, I see," he said, touching Ben on the shoulder.

I heard Mrs. Goring cackle from off screen as the door to Fort Eden slammed shut, a sharp 'HA!' followed by a slam. And I had to agree. Ben was saying one thing by nodding yes to Rainsford. But his hands told a different story as he made and released fists, trying to work the stiffness out of his fingers.

"Mrs. Goring has been my helper for many, many years," Rainsford said, nodding toward the front door where she'd exited. "She's not nearly as mean as she wants all of you to believe. In fact, if one of you was drowning in the pond, she'd be the first to dive in after you. Just ask Davis."

"Really?" Avery asked, trying to calculate exactly what the remark meant.

"Really," Rainsford concluded, and moved forward three or four steps, turning to face them as one. "It's uncommon for two people to be cured at once, but not entirely unprecedented. Sometimes it's a comfort to have a friend."

"It's not that," Connor said defiantly. "I just don't want to wait anymore and neither does he."

"Is this true, Alex?"

Alex confirmed with a loud yes, but I think that if he could have been truthful, he would have agreed more with Rainsford. Alex Hersch didn't want to go alone, whatever going alone meant.

Everyone fanned out except Rainsford and the two guys, the three of them standing close in a circle as Rainsford said something I couldn't hear. This went on for a minute or so, and then Rainsford and Alex and Connor all went through the doorway. On the other side, they'd find the black curtain, and then Kino would guide them to the elevator. Apparently Alex and Connor didn't have any interest in talking to Dr. Stevens first, or they'd already done it earlier in the day. I thought about that and cycled back to the boys' quarters.

"How'd I miss that?" I said, because something had changed. They'd both been in there all right, because the 3 and 4 on the back wall had been painted through. The 3 was slashed over with the color green, the 4 with the color orange.

"So Alex is green and Connor is orange," I said, eating a stack of three crackers and chasing them with water. I felt as if I was in a movie theater, eating a snack as I waited for the show to start. Maybe it was because I'd become jaded in the bomb shelter, or possibly it was because I didn't really know Connor or Alex. Whatever the cause, I didn't feel sorry for these guys. If anything, I was experiencing a sense of wonderment. *What's going to happen? How badly are these two going to get the juice?*

I imagined Keith in his room, mowing down other players in a video game, bodies all over the place.

Now we're talking!

You know, Keith, this probably isn't good for your brain.

Sure it is! Look how much fun I'm having!

I stood in the bomb shelter waiting, wishing Keith was standing there with me. He'd be all into it, which would make it seem okay.

These dudes are gonna fry—the suspense is killing me!

I know, right? Hey Keith, I bet this one will have dogs.

Dogs?

Yeah, mean ones. And I bet they'll be huge.

Sweet. Give me some of those crackers, bro.

The center screen had taken on an almost ghostly quality as I waited. Everyone seemed to have gone completely numb, sitting around as if they were praying or falling asleep. Marisa, again, was nowhere. I knew she was staying up late a lot, too afraid to sleep at night. Probably she was sleeping, but it bothered me not seeing her among the others.

I pulled out my Recorder and opened the photographs I'd shot early this morning, the ones that had to do with Connor and Alex. A quick look at the doors first, then I swiped forward to the long, skinny shots of the walls with their bizarre paintings. Alex Hersch's wall was covered with horrific wild dogs, their eyes wide and rabid.

The dogs crested like waves as they crashed against one another, searching for something to sink their teeth into. The other wall, Connor's, was in the same style but paneled across like a comic strip. Four panels, all of the same image: buildings, morbidly intertwined like tangled rope, twisting as if down an unseen drain a thousand feet below. On the first panel, the silhouette of a body falling through the center of the scene, and in each panel that followed the body getting smaller and smaller. The panels made my head feel dizzy and I turned away, checking my watch. 5:00 PM. The witching hour, it turned out, for two monitors began to glow. They were monitors that hadn't turned on before, so I knew they belonged to Connor Bloom and Alex Hersch.

A morbid curiosity passed through me and I glanced back and forth between the screens as if they were projecting reality shows gone horribly wrong.

Alex had gotten through the doorway and stopped moving, his dark eyes wide with surprise. If I hadn't known better I would have said someone had driven nails through his shirt sleeves and pant legs. He was literally pinned to the wall with fear, staring at the other side of the green room, where two rotting dog houses sat next to each other. Both were huge, their black doorways staring back at Alex like the hollow eyes of a monster about to wake up and rip the world apart. The helmet sat on the stone floor of the room, halfway between the dog houses and Alex Hersch, its tangle of wires and tubes lifting into the ceiling.

My attention turned to the other monitor, where things weren't going any better for Connor Bloom.

Some people probably find it entertaining to watch an otherwise brash young athlete being brought down a notch or two. But there was nothing fun about watching Connor Bloom step into the orange room and crumple to the floor. I thought I might enjoy a small moment of superiority—*Hey, big man on campus, welcome to my world. This is how you make people feel when you pick on them. How's life treating you now, huh?*—but there was none of that, not even a glimmer of satisfaction. If this place could put Connor Bloom on the floor that fast, I wondered what it could do to me if Rainsford ever figured out where I was hiding.

What had brought Connor to his knees was a ladder, one of the kind that opens up and stands on its own like an upside-down *V*. It was sitting in the middle of the orange room splattered with orange paint, and at the top sat the helmet. He'd have to climb six rungs in order to reach the top, where, I guessed, he would be required to sit down and put on the helmet.

From this point on my eyes took turns moving between the two monitors as they flashed and crackled with life. Soon enough both Connor and Alex had gathered enough courage to make their individual journeys to the helmets, undoubtedly helped by the whispering voice I'd blocked out on my own visit below Fort Eden.

I watched as Connor and Alex endured dueling nightmares, taking turns on an expedition into madness.

Connor, I knew, was so afraid of heights that he'd begun having trouble with even the most basic related tasks, such as going up a flight of stairs at school or a set of bleachers at a football game. The screens popped wildly, going back and forth between the orange room and the scene inside the helmet. On the screen itself, the words and the orange mercury line appeared.

Connor Bloom, 15
Acute fear: falling

Connor Bloom's muscular forearms were held in a tight flex as he gripped the edges of the ladder; and as the screen changed to what he saw, I could understand why. He was still on the ladder, looking down at his own feet, but the floor in the room had begun falling away. The four legs of the ladder sat precariously close to what remained of the floor, a three-foot-square pillar of stone. Outside the helmet, a cable with a hook had dropped from the ceiling, which Connor reached out for blindly. A moment later, it was clipped to the back of his leather belt. He seemed to calm down a notch, glancing up and finding the cable hooked into the ceiling along with all the wires and tubes from the helmet. The scene went back inside the helmet, where the floor around the ladder continued to slowly fall away, now twenty feet below in the shadows.

I could relate to Alex Hersch's fear as I switched my attention to his monitor, because I'd been cornered by two crazy dogs out at my grandfather's farm in Northern California. I remember thinking they were going to rip me apart before I scaled the metal fence they'd pinned me against and ran away.

Alex Hersch, 15
Acute fear: dogs

The green line appeared at the edge of the screen,

and, shockingly, it was already halfway to the finish line. Alex had barely even put on the helmet and already he was rounding the bend for home. Bits and pieces from sessions I'd listened to drifted into my mind as I watched Alex. His back was against the wall again, as far away from the dog houses as he could get without running from the room.

You should let your family buy you a dog, Alex. It will help.

No, it won't.

Of course it will. You had one bad experience a long time ago. Not all dogs are like that.

What about a cat instead? Could we start there? Or a hamster.

A hamster isn't going to cure you, Alex.

Then I don't want to be cured.

The word looked so harmless on the screen. *Dogs*. I imagined or hoped for a toy poodle and a Chihuahua to step out of the dog houses and nip at Alex's feet, but that was, of course, not to be. These were not small dogs. They were not friendly or eager to be petted. I saw their snouts first, which were accompanied by a black symphony of low, growling sounds. When their heads emerged together, I felt truly sorry for Alex Hersch. They were huge animals, their mouths dripping with saliva, their bodies covered in matted hair. When they began to growl and snarl, the monitor switched to Alex in the room, who was clawing at the closed door, trying to escape from the green room. A second later the scene was back on the dogs, which were moving closer, cornering Alex, teeth bared. They attacked together, a mad leap and the sound of the world being torn apart.

And that was it for Alex Hersch. The green line was already at the top. He was flooded with fear, the wires dancing over his head. After that, he lay slouched in the corner of the room and the dogs were gone.

Only Connor's scene remained, and it was about to head into overdrive as I stepped closer. Suddenly, the floor wasn't just falling slowly away in the helmet; it was racing. It had the unnerving effect of making it feel as if Connor Bloom was rising up in the air at the same time, the distance between the ladder and the bottom of the room growing. Given how scary I knew this must have been for Connor, it was surprising to see that the orange line was only a quarter of the way up the side of the screen.

This guy is tough. Maybe the room can't break him.

I should have known better. The floor blasted back to where it was with a grinding noise of rocks and metal. The floor had changed while it was away, growing talons and spears reaching up into the middle of the room. The floor stayed only a moment, just long enough for Connor to get a really good look at how things would be when he fell, and then it was falling again. This time one of the four legs of the ladder was left without a solid footing; and in the helmet, the world began to wobble. As if this wasn't plenty of ammunition to finish off someone afraid of falling, the cable that had once been attached to the ceiling broke free, dangling uselessly from Connor's belt. Inside the world of the helmet, Connor Bloom had to be thinking: *I am no longer connected to anything. It's just me and a three-legged ladder now.*

The scene on the screen shifted to the orange room, where the orange line had reached the midway point. Nothing had changed, and I understood once more that life inside the helmet was very different from life outside. What Connor saw was an altered reality, presented by a madman bent on driving irrational fear off a cliff. The room was, simply, the same. The cable was still attached to the ceiling, and the ladder sat firmly on the concrete floor; but Connor had no way of knowing this. The orange line was moving fast now, nearing the top. As my monitor returned to the scene in the helmet, Connor Bloom lost his balance. The ladder tipped, and the orange line found its end. He was falling.

The power of a dual cure left me nervous and upset, a sick adrenaline pumping through my veins; but it wasn't until the very end that I was finally forced to turn away from the monitors. Connor Bloom's orange room was back. The ladder lay tipped over on the floor like a dead animal. Connor had fallen, but the cable attached to his belt had held. His arms and legs were splayed out in the air as if he was held up by many wires, and the helmet was still on. All those wires and tubes and the cable—something about seeing him hanging there rigid, like rigor mortis was already setting in, made me rip the headphones off my head and gasp for air.

I shut my eyes, but the image remained.

When at last I looked back at the wall, Connor Bloom and Alex Hersch were gone.

MARISA

An hour after Connor Bloom and Alex Hersch were cured, Mrs. Goring drove the metal cart down the ramp and I dialed the light off just as she threw open the door to the basement. She was in a foul mood.

"Damn this place and these stupid kids!" she yelled. I got the feeling that she viewed the basement, on occasion, as a place where her deepest frustrations could be expressed in peace. It was a place where she could scream and no one would hear her.

She banged the cart loudly into one of the metal shelves, knocking cans onto the floor. One of them bounced, then rolled in my general direction. There was nothing I could do but stand in the corner of the darkened bomb shelter and hope she didn't feel compelled to pick up the can. She picked up all the cans but the one, which had rolled all the way to the bomb shelter door. Mrs. Goring was angrily muttering half-formed words as she set each can back on the shelf. I'd cleaned up the room and put my things in my backpack, and I knew the room well enough to move with only the sliver of light from the basement leaking in.

I knelt down, quietly sliding on the slick concrete and under the cot, until I was as far against the wall as possible. I reached out my hand and grabbed my backpack, pulling it toward me. It was thick in the middle with Clif Bars and water bottles and clothes I'd stuffed inside, so it caught on the metal edge of the cot. The busted wheel on Mrs. Goring's cart started flopping toward the bomb shelter door. She was moving like a crazy woman in a grocery store, mowing down whatever stood in her way. She slammed the cart against the wall outside the door, and it bounced off its wheels.

"Oh, for God's sake," she said, having tipped the

empty cart over on its side. I pushed up on the old springs and lifted the edge of the cot an inch off the ground, silently sliding my pack in under the cot with me. I was pretty sure she'd be able to see me hiding if the lights were turned on, but there was no place else to go. All I could do was stay still and hope she didn't ram the cart into the rickety old cot.

It was quiet in the basement—too quiet—and I started to feel claustrophobic. If Mrs. Goring was going to find me, I sure didn't want to be trapped. I needed to be up on my feet so I could knock her down and run for the exit. I started to slide out from under the cot, but the door to the bomb shelter moved and I froze in place. Light from the basement grew brighter, and Mrs. Goring stepped inside the bomb shelter. I saw her boots, scuffed leather rimmed with black rubber soles. She was staring at the wall of monitors.

I imagined her standing with one can of corn in each hand, prepared to use them as weapons if she needed them; but then I heard her clicking the buttons on the wall, searching for images. There was nothing—the system had gone dead and hadn't returned after Connor and Alex were cured—and this bothered her.

"I hate this place," she said, and then I heard a crashing sound that made me wince under the springs. A heavy object hit the concrete floor, bouncing sideways into the bomb shelter door. When it hit the floor again, I saw it for an instant—the heavy can she'd picked up—and then it was flying up and out of my field of vision. It bounced once more, rolled in my direction. The can didn't stop until it was resting against my hip.

"I feel much better," she said. It sounded like she was still facing the wall of monitors, observing her handiwork, and I silently pushed the can so that it rolled back out into the openness of the room. A second passed, maybe two, then her big boot was on the can, kicking it out the door and into the basement. She followed, picked up her cart, and went back to whatever it was she had been doing.

The bomb shelter door was swung wide-open, and I could see Mrs. Goring's shadow on the floor out there, gathering supplies for something awful she intended to cook for dinner. I stuck my head out from under the cot and looked at the wall: Ben Dugan's monitor, the one at the top, was filled with a spidery burst of glass. She'd thrown the can right into the wall, smashing one of the seven screens.

It was Mrs. Goring's habit, I had found, to leave the basement door open if she planned on coming back down again soon. That was the case as she turned off the light, and I listened to her leave.

I have to get out of here or I'll go crazy, I thought, sliding out from under the cot and throwing on my backpack. I gathered what courage I had, which didn't feel like enough, and walked through the basement. At the bottom of the ramp leading up into the Bunker, I hesitated, hearing her rattling pots and pans in the kitchen. But I was determined to get free as I put one foot in front of the other until, miraculously, I stood at the top of the ramp. Around the corner something began to boil, and I heard the sound of Mrs. Goring humming gruffly, then the sound of her spitting.

So gross, so awful, I thought, glad I wasn't on the Fort Eden meal plan.

I was losing my nerve, preparing to go back down the ramp to the bomb shelter and wait out another night, when someone knocked at Mrs. Goring's door.

"Cooking!" she screamed. "Go away!"

The knocking persisted, and she stomped out of the kitchen. My chance had come and I moved quickly, past the pot of boiling water, which appeared to have nothing else in it, and next to the hall that led to the front door.

"What do *you* want?" Mrs. Goring said.

"They sent me on a mission to find dinner. Everyone's starving."

I could tell by the voice that it was Kate Hollander. It was dark in the hall, and I risked creeping from the kitchen to the sitting room; two quick steps and I was safely around the corner.

"Tell your fellow idiots to be patient," Mrs. Goring said. "Rainsford wants dinner at eight sharp, with the lot of you. Deal with it."

"That's like two more hours," Kate complained. She started to ask for a snack to hold them over, and Mrs. Goring slammed the door in her face.

Trust me, Kate, you don't want what she's serving, I thought.

Mrs. Goring was back at the stove swiftly, then grumbling, then heading back down to the basement for something she needed.

By the time she got back to the kitchen I was out the door, across the clearing, and into the woods.

I'd made a decision after watching Connor Bloom's and Alex Hersch's cures, and I was unwavering about seeing it through. I needed answers, and there was only one person I could think of who might be able to help me find them. As I made my way toward the pond, one thought was at the forefront of my mind.

I'm going to find Davis before he finds me.

"Three nights out here. Impressive."

Davis was sitting on the dock when I arrived at the pond. He was staring out over the water, the pipe wrench resting at his feet.

"Yeah, well," I said, staying back far enough that I could run and maybe get away if I needed to. Although really, who was I fooling? Davis was built like a running back. He'd catch me no matter how big a lead I started with.

"I'm not going to tell anyone I found you," Davis said. His back was to me, and he kept staring at the water, waiting for me to come closer.

"You didn't find me," I said. "I found you."

"True enough," he said, and then he glanced over his shoulder and smiled warmly. "I was running out of ideas. You're a damn good hider, Will Besting."

"You have no idea," I offered, thinking of all the times I'd made myself vanish at home or at a mall or at school years ago. I was, I had to agree, a hell of a good hider.

"Doc Stevens is worried about you," said Davis. "So is Rainsford."

"What about the rest? I'm guessing they don't care too much."

"They've got troubles of their own," Davis said. "You know the drill: the world revolves around you and only you at fifteen."

I thought about how Davis was only seventeen, how he wasn't old enough to be saying such things, but I let it pass.

"What's going on inside?" I asked instead. He had to imagine I knew nothing at all.

"People are getting well. You could be getting well, too. All you gotta do is go through the doorway."

I was surprised to find that I'd crept awfully close, within a few feet of the dock itself. The cool grass matted under my shoes, and I heard the crows moving overhead, an early autumn chill settling on the pond.

"How do they get cured?" I asked, wanting to trust him and hoping he'd be honest with me.

He looked out over the water again, contemplating something as the sun began to fall below the tree line on the other side of the water.

"I wish I could tell you," he said. "But the honest-to-god truth is, I have no idea. When I was here a while back, there were the same number of patients, so there must be something about having just the right number of people together, supporting one another. And I remember Rainsford from the first, thinking that he was old and that he couldn't be good for much. *This guy can barely get up the stairs, how is he going to save me?* I thought. I remember that after I met him I started feeling, I don't know, looser, I guess, like I wasn't as uptight, you know?"

Yeah, I thought, *because he is controlling your mind!*

"The cure itself I have no memory of," he went on, breathing in a big gulp of air and releasing it, like he was enjoying the view of the pond so much he could barely stand it. "I went down an elevator—that much I recall—but the rest is missing entirely. All I know is, I can jump in this pond and swim all I want."

"It sounds messed up to me, the way it gets done," I said. "Like it's a trick or something worse."

"I hear you, I really do," Davis said, getting up and taking a step toward me, which caused me to take a step back toward the gloom of the forest. "Look, Will, it just is what it is. It's a cure, a *real* cure. In this case, with the way Rainsford operates, that has to be enough."

"What if it's not?"

Davis looked at me sympathetically, and I realized that I'd had a fairly normal conversation with him. I didn't know him, but I'd been able to talk without losing it. It wasn't completely unheard of, but he was older and better in ways I never would be, which usually set me off. Like Connor Bloom, Mr. Big Man on Campus, Davis had that look: the kind of person who'd gang up with his pals and stuff me in a locker.

"I will say this much," he said, settling down on his haunches and picking at the soft grass. "Since I've been back, the whole thing does seem a little on the strange side. Just tell me this much—are you safe out here? Can you last another day or two if it takes that long? Because if you can't, then I gotta take you in. I wouldn't be able to live with myself if you got hurt."

I thought about what he'd said as I felt the cold begin to chill my face.

"Give me your word you won't say anything, and I'll tell you where I'm hiding."

Davis got up and reached out his hand. There was a large gap of three or four steps between us, but he didn't move. He wasn't going to come any closer and scare me off. I must have looked like a feral cat, slowly coming barely near enough to lean forward and put out my hand.

"I don't even know if you should go in there," Davis said. "It works, but there's absolutely no doubt about it: it's weird."

He shook my hand, promised he wouldn't tell, and smiled as if he was my big brother. It was *so* hard not to trust this guy. He'd been through the program; but more than that, he seemed to understand how I felt. I was coming to the end of my rope, and feeling a deep sense of desperation, I let him in.

"I've been staying in the basement of Mrs. Goring's bunker," I blurted.

"No way," he said, and we both laughed (him first, then me nervously joining in). "You couldn't pay me enough money to sneak in there. Seriously, impressive."

"Do me a favor?" I asked.

"Whatever you need."

"Knock on her front door at a quarter to eight, offer to help carry dinner over through the clearing."

"So you can get back in?" he asked.

"Yeah, so I can get back in."

He nodded and laughed again and asked if I needed anything else.

He had no idea about what was down there, no clue whatsoever that I'd watched people being cured. I had a flash of insight, imagining Davis with the helmet on, images of him falling through the ice on a frozen pond. I couldn't tell him what I knew, but I could at least ask him for a favor before we parted ways.

"Could you check on Marisa for me, let her know I'm doing okay out here?"

He knew instantly that I liked her but didn't make a big deal out of it.

"I'll tell everyone you're fine, just not ready to come in. Rainsford will be the toughest to sell, but it's cool. As long as he knows you're not dead or injured, I think it'll be fine."

The wind rustled through the trees, and we both looked off at the riffling pond.

"Do you think she can be cured?" I asked. There was a part of me that wanted that for her, no matter how horrible it would be.

"I do," he said. "But if you want, I can tell her you don't want her to go through with it."

"Really?"

"Sure I can, but I don't think she'll listen. People around her are being cured. She wants that for herself."

"Yeah, I suppose you're right."

"One last try—you sure you don't want in? This opportunity might not come around again."

"I'm sure," I said, and I was. Nothing could get me down into that hallway and through door number 6. They couldn't make me do it.

"Okay then, let's get you back into Mrs. Goring's basement."

We walked together down the path, then separated as we neared Fort Eden. Twenty minutes later he was knocking on Mrs. Goring's door and she was yelling at him, but he was a persuasive guy for sure. Soon enough they were carrying the food over in cardboard boxes, and I was passing through a clearing at twilight.

When I got back to the bomb shelter, it was after 8:00 PM and, missing Marisa, I started thinking unreasonable thoughts.

Maybe I should just give up. I could be there for her. She'd like that.

But I couldn't do it. I was afraid of what would happen to me. But more than that, I was afraid of being in the room upstairs with all those people.

I was alone, and that was how things were going to stay.

By 11:00 PM I was convinced that Mrs. Goring had broken the entire system by throwing a can of beets at the wall (I'd found the can in question, dented and alone on the floor in the basement). The bubble of glass on Ben Dugan's monitor hadn't shattered out into the bomb shelter but stayed, like a broken windshield, and so I'd taken off my shoes without fear of stepping on a shard of glass. I got so frustrated at the blankness before me that I kicked the narrow bedpost and managed to stub my middle toe. I'd gotten hurt before trying to inflict punishment on inanimate objects. It was, I guess, a hobby of mine.

I sat on the cot rubbing my toe and thought about the lawnmower in our garage, which sometimes took fifty pulls to start. The mower was a common recipient of my wrath; but it gave as good as it got, exacting scuffs and bruises. Its blank metal silence only made me angrier. Berzerk, with its menacing 2D robots, could also be particularly frustrating. At least with the Atari

I could throw the controller or pound my fist on the game console when I got axed on the screen, both of which I did all the time.

I was sitting on the cot, thinking of the mower and the Atari and my injured toe, when the main monitor sputtered to life. As it did, a line of smoke peeled out through the cracks in Ben Dugan's monitor and up the white wall.

"That can't be good," I said out loud, positioning the oversized monkey phones over my ears. I'd started calling them monkey phones on the off chance that it might amuse me, which it didn't.

The wisp of smoke became a thin line and vanished, but there was no mistaking the smell: burned plastic. Something was shorting out behind Ben's monitor, threatening to catch fire and cook the entire system. I couldn't help thinking that a bomb shelter was supposed to be the safest place on Earth when, in reality, a fire in the basement would more than likely kill me with ruthless efficiency.

At least for the moment, the smoke was gone and the smell evaporated in the air. Looking at the main screen in the center of the wall, I saw Rainsford seated at the table, where I could make out his profile. He was at least seventy, with deep lines across his forehead and a gray widow's peak on top of his head. He appeared to be playing a game of backgammon with Alex Hersch while the other boys watched. Their words were faint, so far from the camera, and they all three had on the same kind of T-shirts: white with the letter *E*. The whole camp T-shirt idea felt hokey and unnecessary; but all the same, I was dying to have one.

"What's the rule on that again?" Connor asked, glaring at the board with what appeared to be confusion.

"Splitting the number is fine, but he can't land there or there," said Rainsford, pointing to various places on the board I couldn't see.

"Dang it," Alex said, shaking his leg in the space beside the round table.

"Dude, your feet are messed up," said Connor.

"It's just this one, keeps falling asleep," said Alex. "It's the pinpricking that really bugs me."

"Give it a day or two," said Rainsford, a soft but commanding tone I'd grown used to. "You'll be right as rain."

Connor wobbled a little at the table, as if he was drunk; and I wondered if they'd given him a sedative to calm him down after the cure. He started to get up, but Rainsford touched his hand.

"Better stay here a while longer, then early to bed."

"That's a good idea," Connor agreed, settling back heavily in his chair. "I think I'll watch you finish off Alex."

Ben had been sitting there writing a letter, but he'd stopped, shaking his hand like writing was putting a profound strain on his fingers.

Everyone that's been cured has come back with an ailment, I thought.

They seemed like minor things: Kate with her headaches; these guys with their hand, foot, and dizziness problems. Strange, but knowing what they'd been through, reasonable side effects. Maybe it was like chemotherapy, when the patient's hair falls out. Eventually the hair grows back. Sooner or later these people would stop having odd little problems.

The three girls came out of their quarters all together, and Rainsford crooked his neck to watch them as they settled onto the couch on the far end of the room. It was dark in that corner, but I could make out their shadows and hear them talking with Rainsford and the boys.

Avery sat nearest to the table, fidgeting as if she wanted to say something but couldn't bring herself to do it.

"Is there something on your mind, Avery?" Rainsford asked. He shook the dice for the game and threw them on the board, absently making his move. Avery looked stricken, like she'd been caught in front of everyone doing something that wasn't allowed. Kate bumped up against her shoulder. The two of them had obviously talked, and Kate was either trying to offer solidarity or trick Avery into saying something she shouldn't.

"Did you and Davis have a fight?"

Avery's question turned every head in the room. Her words were sharp, very unlike her.

"A difference of opinion, nothing more," said Rainsford. "In any case, his work was through here. It was time for him to go."

"I can't believe Will is out there and he won't come in," Kate said. News of Davis's discovery had reached everyone. "What a nut job."

Ouch. That one stung, and I hoped Marisa would come to my rescue. But she was in a sullen mood, thoughtful and quiet.

"But why did he have to leave so suddenly? I barely got to say good-bye. Can't you invite him back for breakfast in the morning?" Avery pleaded.

"Avery, you're being pathetic," Connor said.

"Shut up."

"Just sayin', everyone knows you like the guy. Just text him when you get home; what's the big deal?"

Avery pulled her knees to her chest and sulked, and Kate bore down on Connor with her violently blue eyes, an arm thrown around Avery's shoulder.

"Jeez, mellow out, you two," said Connor. "It ain't seventh grade."

Alex and Ben looked torn about who they should side with—the pretty girls or the top dog—and chose instead to ignore the situation completely.

The room grew quiet and uninteresting, so I picked up *The Woman in the Dunes*. The bomb shelter was an ideal reading spot, with its good light and dead silence; and I'd reached the halfway point in the book earlier in the day. There were some disturbing coincidences in the plot line. In the story, an entomologist is lured down a ladder to the bottom of a deep sand dune on the promise that a rare insect is nesting there. When he steps into the sand, someone removes the ladder, and he finds a woman living at the bottom of the dune. She's spent her entire life shoveling sand out of the hole, which I still don't quite understand; and he's trapped down there, forced to help her for the rest of his sorry life.

Maybe it was the late hour or the confines of the bomb shelter or the fact that I was trapped like the man in the story. Or maybe it was the fact that Mrs. Goring, while she doesn't know I'm here, had control over my comings and goings. Whatever the reasons, the book was bothering me, so I turned on my Recorder instead and listened to old audio sessions from Dr. Stevens's office as I waited for the main room to clear out.

Ten or fifteen minutes later, at about 11:30 PM, Avery went alone into the girls' quarters and I switched views. She sat in the chair—the numbers 5 and 7 still clearly visible on the wall behind her—and began talking to Dr. Stevens.

I don't care about anything any more.

Why do you say that? Did something happen?

No, nothing. I just don't care.

I see.

Do you know . . .

Avery trailed off.

What, Avery? What is it?

Do you know how I can get in touch with Davis?

He was a patient of mine a few years back, but I don't think—

I just want to talk to him.

It's technically not something I'm supposed to do, give out patient information.

I know; it's just—I think Rainsford chased him off. I don't think he wants me talking to him.

Do you have feelings for him?

Who? Rainsford? God, no.

Davis. Do you have feelings for Davis?

He understands why I can't be cured.

You mean you told him?

Avery shrugged, not willing to say.

Talk to Rainsford. He'll know what to do.

But he won't listen.

Talk to him, before it's too late.

Too late for what?

Avery, we're nearing the end. Your chance to be cured is about to pass.

I can't be cured.

You can.

You don't know what you're talking about.

Avery got up and walked out of the room. But when she did, as an act of defiance or I don't know what, she dunked a paintbrush in a can of paint I couldn't see and violently wiped out both the 5 and the 7.

There, the look said. *Happy now? Leave me alone.*

And then she was gone, and the room was empty. It seemed like a bad omen, both numbers destroyed on the wall; and stranger still, the paint she'd used was white. The 5 was hit the hardest: a thick glob obliterating the number. But by the time her stroke had reached the 7, the paint was thin and the 7 showed through. It was a red number 7; and it looked for all the world as if it was fighting its way out of the white, unwilling to be destroyed so easily.

I pushed the button for the main room and watched as nothing very interesting happened: Rainsford and the boys playing a meaningless game at the table, the girls checked out on the couch. It began to feel as if Rainsford was babysitting or waiting for something important to happen, the game only a prop, a deceptive reason to stay.

My mind began to question: *What had Davis said to Rainsford? And what about Davis and Avery?* Even I knew they liked each other; it was obvious just from looking at their body language when they were together. Maybe Davis had discovered something bad about the program and been asked to leave.

I paced back and forth in the bomb shelter and took off the headphones, tossing them on the cot. Scratching at the sides of my head, I started to have a conviction about Marisa.

I can't let her go through with it. I can't.

I'd have gladly stayed sick my whole life in exchange for having Marisa cured. But how could this be right? The depth of the basement of rooms, the bizarre treatments, the whole crazy mess—cure or no cure, I had to get to Marisa as fast as I could. I had to convince her not to go through with it. And then we had to get away.

I don't know how many minutes passed while I had these thoughts—three, five, ten? In the stillness of the bomb shelter, time seemed to stand still like that sometimes. It made me wonder what a prison would feel like, how time would begin to have no meaning at all; and it scared me. What if I never escaped the clearing and Fort Eden? What if this entire thing was designed to keep us prisoner, like the bug-man at the bottom of the dune in the story?

I put the headphones on and glanced back at the main room, which had become surprisingly empty in the few minutes since I'd left it. The last of the guys were going through the doorway to their room, Rainsford was nowhere to be found, and Marisa was sitting in the dark-shadowed corner on the far couch. She was curled up in a ball; and if I had to guess, I would have said she was crying.

Give it at least fifteen minutes, Will. Make sure they're down for the night, I thought.

My watch read almost midnight, a little early for everyone to turn in; but then Connor and Alex were the noisiest of the group, and they'd been cured earlier in the day. They'd be tired. Avery was upset, and Kate had become her confidante; probably they were sitting across from each other on one of the beds, whispering about Davis and cures and headaches. That left Marisa, who was like me, all alone now.

Seven minutes later I couldn't stand it. I didn't even clean things up this time. I didn't care.

I threw on my backpack—the food and the water I had left would come in handy—and I turned for the door.

I was going up there and getting Marisa, and the two of us were leaving Fort Eden.

Opening the door to Fort Eden proved scarier than I'd imagined it would be. Plotting my escape and planning to take another participant with me made me feel as if Rainsford was my enemy. I hadn't fully thought of him in that way before; but now, staring into the gloom, I felt his furious gaze from the deepest part of the fort.

Something wasn't right. Something was off. What was it? With only the faintest light to guide my steps, I searched my mind for what was wrong.

What did I miss? What does he know?

I held my Recorder in my hand, with my finger on the PLAY button. If I heard whispering or garbled voices, I'd be listening to Marisa's favorite song before any kind of mind tricks could be played on me. I could get to the couch and give Marisa one earbud and we could listen together. How insanely romantic would that be? The very thought of it got me moving faster along the floor. I stopped caring. We were going to escape, us two, out the door and into the night. We'd listen to "I Wanna Be Adored" while we shivered in the woods, and the only thing to keep us warm would be each other. I was lost in this ridiculous dream when I reached the couch and discovered my mistake.

It wasn't Marisa curled up in a ball on the couch but Avery Varone, who looked up at me with tears in her eyes.

"*Will?*"

I pushed the button on my Recorder completely by accident, and the music began to play, soft and slow. It was a quiet song at the start, and I could hear Avery's voice.

"Oh, my God, *Will*, it is you."

In the time that I'd taken my eyes off the screen and decided to escape with Marisa, she'd gone to bed and been replaced by Avery.

"Hi," I said, and felt as if there was a potato stuck in my throat.

"Sit down, it's okay," she said, wiping away mascara that had run down her cheeks. She was a pretty girl—not Kate Hollander, but pretty just the same. She had a desolate beauty up close, like an empty field of rolling hills.

"I thought you were someone else," I said, turning off the music and taking out the earbuds. Thank God I hadn't put up my hoodie or she might have thought I was an executioner come to take her away.

"Who?" she asked. "Who did you think I was?"

"I thought you were Marisa," I said. I was starting to shake, wondering what it would be like if everyone else came out of their rooms and found me here. They'd slash me apart with their words. Connor Bloom might even hit me. It could happen.

And then there was Avery herself.

I'm not sure she can be trusted.

Don't be ridiculous. Of course she can. She'll play her part; I'll see to it.

Were Dr. Stevens and Rainsford talking about Avery, or someone else?

"You don't need to worry," Avery said. "I'm not going to tell. Davis said you might turn up. It's why I waited."

This was a curious comment, and curiosity has a way of putting my sizzling brain to rest. It's like two giant question marks can't fit inside my head at the same time. I was considering what might happen if a group of my peers gathered around me, but I was also hopelessly interested in what Avery meant.

Curiosity won and I sat down.

"Where have you been?" asked Avery.

"In the basement of the bunker," I replied. "What

happened between Davis and Rainsford?" I asked.

"I don't know," Avery said, turning away as if the words were so frustrating they were making her want to scream. "He wouldn't tell me, and then he was just gone."

"Gone?" I asked.

She nodded fast a couple of times, wiped away another falling tear.

"Did you ask Rainsford what happened?"

"I did. He said something about Davis being gone because his work was done here. I think they had a fight."

I repeated what the others had said—she could still get in touch with him if she wanted to.

"I guess."

It was a hollow reply, like she didn't know any better what to say or she was just too emotionally spent to care.

I glanced over my shoulder at all the doors in the room, wondering when Marisa would come back out. But that wasn't going to happen until everyone was asleep, and Avery Varone was still out here.

"Do you think the cures work?" I asked.

"Yeah, they work," she said.

"Then why won't you do it?"

She rolled her eyes and laughed in a way that

was filled with regret.

"I say it, but no one listens."

"You can't be cured," I offered.

She nodded, then leaned her head back on the soft leather couch, staring at the shadows on the ceiling.

"I'm sorry," I said. "If it's any consolation, we almost share something in common."

"What's that?" she asked, her neck still tilted back but her head turning to me now.

"You can't be cured, and I *won't* be cured. I think this entire thing is insane."

"Could be," she said thoughtfully. "It doesn't really matter either way."

"Listen, Avery, I think I'm going to leave now. Please don't tell anyone I was here or where I've been."

"I won't," she said. "And, Will?"

"Yeah?"

"She likes you. She told me so."

Avery Varone was incurably romantic. She was falling for Davis and paying attention to others falling around her. My heart fluttered—*she likes me?* I had a moment of feeling it was too good to be true. It was a moment that was not to last.

"Speaking of Marisa," I said. "Usually she's the last one up. Where is she?"

"I thought you knew," said Avery. And then Avery said three words I will never forget as long as I live.

"She's being cured."

I didn't believe Avery Varone when she said she wouldn't tell. How could she keep a secret like that? I could already hear the conversation with Rainsford.

I know where Will Besting is.

Do you, now.

I do. I'll tell you if you give me Davis's number.

A fair arrangement. Have you a pen?

Sadly, as far as I was concerned, Avery was already under Fort Eden's spell, so more likely it would go something like this:

I know where Will Besting is.

Tell me. Now.

Basement, Mrs. Goring's bunker.

Go away.

Yes, sir.

I thought these things as I ran down the extended tunnel between the fort and the Bunker. I thought them as I entered the bomb shelter and set the huge monkey phones on my ears, felt the soft sting of the cracked plastic on my skin.

I wasn't someone who prayed very often, mostly because I didn't understand what I was doing. But I prayed that night in the Bunker, or did something like praying as I waited for Marisa's monitor to turn on.

I know I said I wouldn't listen. I said I wouldn't watch, but I'm not doing this because I want to. I'm doing it so you don't have to go through it alone. I'm right here. Please, God, if you have any heart at all, let her know she's not alone. I'm here. I'm here. I'm here.

I was whispering the words, hearing them muffled in my head, wishing the monitor would never turn on. Maybe Avery was wrong, or maybe she'd lied in order to get me back down here so I'd be trapped.

I'm here, I'm here, I'm here.

I'd listened to Marisa's audio sessions with Dr. Stevens so many times that they were like memorized songs I could return to whenever I wanted; and waiting, the words drifted into my mind.

Do you ever go back?

You mean home?

Yes, home. Do you ever go to Mexico?

No, never.

Can you think of why this might be so?

Because people will judge me. They'll think of me as something I'm not.

You speak perfect English, Marisa. No one's going to judge you for visiting home.

Hablo español mejor que inglés.

You speak Spanish and English.

I speak Spanish better than I do English. I just don't want to.

But why, Marisa? It's a beautiful language. And Mexico—it's your heritage.

Do we have to talk about this?

There's a connection here, Marisa. Why have you abandoned your history?

I don't know.

Does it have anything to do with what happened to your father? Marisa? What happened to him wasn't your fault.

Déjame en paz.

No, I won't leave you alone.

You must.

But I won't. What are you afraid of, Marisa?

I knew what Marisa feared. She was convinced that someone was in her house, trying to take her away. He would take her in the dark while everyone else slept. It kept her awake at night as she stared at the doors in her room: the bathroom door, the closet door, the door from the small family room. Often she would sit on her bed at night and cry, but she was too afraid to speak or call out. She was sure someone was in her room, and always there was the burlap bag.

You're practically a grown-up, Marisa. I don't think they make burlap bags that large.

I think they do.

When you're really afraid—when you're flooding with fear—the man is holding the bag?

Yes, he's at one of the doors, holding the bag. He says he's going to put me in it.

Are you sure about that part?

It's a big bag, big enough for three of me at least. He says he's going to put me inside.

Are you sure?

Why do you keep asking me that?

Because I want to know about the bag.

I told you about the bag.

Who's in the bag, Marisa?

Estoy en la bolsa. I am in the bag.

Are you absolutely sure?

I waited, thinking about Kino and *The Pearl*. Why was he so dead set on rising up? Couldn't he see all it would cost him? And why was Marisa so focused on being as not-Mexican as possible? Every person I'd ever met from that part of the world was friendly and relaxed, full of life, interesting. What was the big deal?

I waited, the humming in my ears starting to bother me.

This is a setup, I thought. *Any second now, Mrs. Goring will be at the door. She's going to murder me with a can of corn. She'll beat me to death with it. She's a very angry woman. She could do it.*

And then, just like that, the waiting was over.

Marisa's monitor was below and to the left of the one in the middle of the group. It fluttered to life magically, softer than the others had: a white room with a glowing edge like an angel's halo.

Maybe God heard me, I thought, adjusting the headphones so they sat right over my ears.

There was something very odd about this room, but I

couldn't put my finger on it. And then I realized: there was no helmet with its ghastly wires and tubes, just a white room and a white door that opened.

Marisa put her head through the doorway, and for a moment I thought she might turn back. It also crossed my mind that a true friend would have gone down there and gotten her. I felt small and worthless, like I'd let her down when she needed me most. She stepped through the doorway; and when she closed it, the nightmare began.

The room went from all white to completely black at the click of the latch, all but the thing that lay on the floor with the wires and the tubes. The helmet was there, stark white against the blackness all around it, glowing as if it was filled with neon light. The light fell on Marisa's face and gave her a pale, hollowed-out quality as she picked up the awful device and held it over her head.

You are adored, I said, closing my eyes.

It was the only prayer I could think of.

Marisa Sorrento, 15
Acute fear: being kidnapped

The monitor in the bomb shelter lit up with what was being shown inside the helmet. Marisa was someplace I had never seen before. It was very dark, the faintest light coming from down long rows of boxes. A man, brown skinned and smiling, with a thick black mustache, held a little girl's hand, pulling her along. When he spoke, it was in broken English, thick with a Spanish accent.

Marisa, come, I show you. Mas grande de setas.

Speak English, Papa. You know how angry they get.

Sí, inglés. Come, Marisa. Follow me. We go to the big mushrooms.

Back in the room, Marisa had knelt on the floor, which bothered me. Was she praying? I think she was. The white line along the right side of the screen began to rise, and the image switched back to inside the helmet.

The long, wooden boxes were filled with mushrooms. She was underground, in some sort of plant where they were growing thousands upon thousands of mushrooms. What could it possibly mean?

You there! Come here—this guy needs a hand moving boxes.

A voice from down the long row, calling Marisa's father away. He turned to her, told her to stay where she was. He would be right back.

There seemed to be a moment in which the little girl started to search and became lost, calling for her papa. When the screen softly filtered back to the room, Marisa hadn't moved. But the white line had. It was nearing halfway.

Well, hello there, Marisa Sorrento. What brings you down here in the dark?

Back inside the helmet now, Marisa turning fast to the voice. A different man, a bad man, holding a flashlight under his face in the way that men do to scare kids at a campout. He wore a cowboy hat, and his pale face shimmered with sweat.

Stay put now, don't go running off on me.

"Run, Marisa! Run!" I yelled in the bomb shelter.

Your daddy needs to shut his mouth, understand?

The helmet nodded up and down.

A strike won't do. Can't have it. Tell me you understand.

I do. A small voice of a five- or six-year-old, afraid.

You see this here bag, Marisa Sorrento?

The giant burlap bag, flopping over the side of the bad man's leg, and the helmet nodding once more.

You get your daddy to shut up, and I won't put him inside. He shuts up, they all shut up. It's all on you. Understand what I'm saying?

The monitor moved to the darkened room, where the white line moved faster, past halfway, into the realm of gushing fear.

When the screen returned to inside the helmet, Marisa was in a bedroom, *her* bedroom, I imagined, and the hour was late. The image had taken on a bluish night security camera glow, and in the glow an empty doorway. The image fluttered, and the empty doorway was filled with a man who wore a cowboy hat. Next to him, a giant burlap bag, filled and heavy.

I got your daddy in this here bag. You wanna take a look?

Go away!

Come on, take a look in here.

Leave me alone!

You should have listened to me, Marisa Sorrento. It's your fault he's in here.

The man moved toward the bed, opening the bag, and Marisa stared into the gaping black hole.

The monitor switched to the room at the bottom of Fort Eden, which had turned entirely white again. I couldn't even see the line, wiped out by all things white; but I knew it had happened. Marisa was flooded with fear, and the wires were jumping to life.

All the while, she never moved. She had knelt and prayed from the start.

I stood in the bomb shelter and felt tears running down my face, her staggering courage breaking my heart in two.

When the monitor went dead and she was gone, I felt more alone than I'd ever felt before and vowed right then and there to leave Mrs. Goring's basement. I would go down the elevator and into room number 5, and I would take her out of this terrible place forever. They could try and stop me, but I'd find a way.

When I turned for the door, I had my first inkling that something was very, very wrong. The door to the bomb shelter wobbled strangely, as if a hard wind was shaking it on its hinges. The headphones, big and clumsy on my head, felt suddenly tighter on my aching ears. From behind the door, Mrs. Goring appeared, a look of wonder on her face, as if something special was about to happen.

And then she spoke, her voice booming past the headphones and into my naked ears.

"Time to get cured, Will Besting!"

She hurled the door shut with a stunning slam that knocked me off my feet and onto the cot. The air in the room turned warm and wet in the darkness, and I fumbled for the light dial, spinning it hard.

The light in the room had changed, a bloody shade of violet, and somehow I just knew.

These headphones are my helmet, plugged into the wall with three wide cords.

This room is my room, sealed away in the basement of Mrs. Goring's bunker.

I was about to be cured whether I liked it or not.

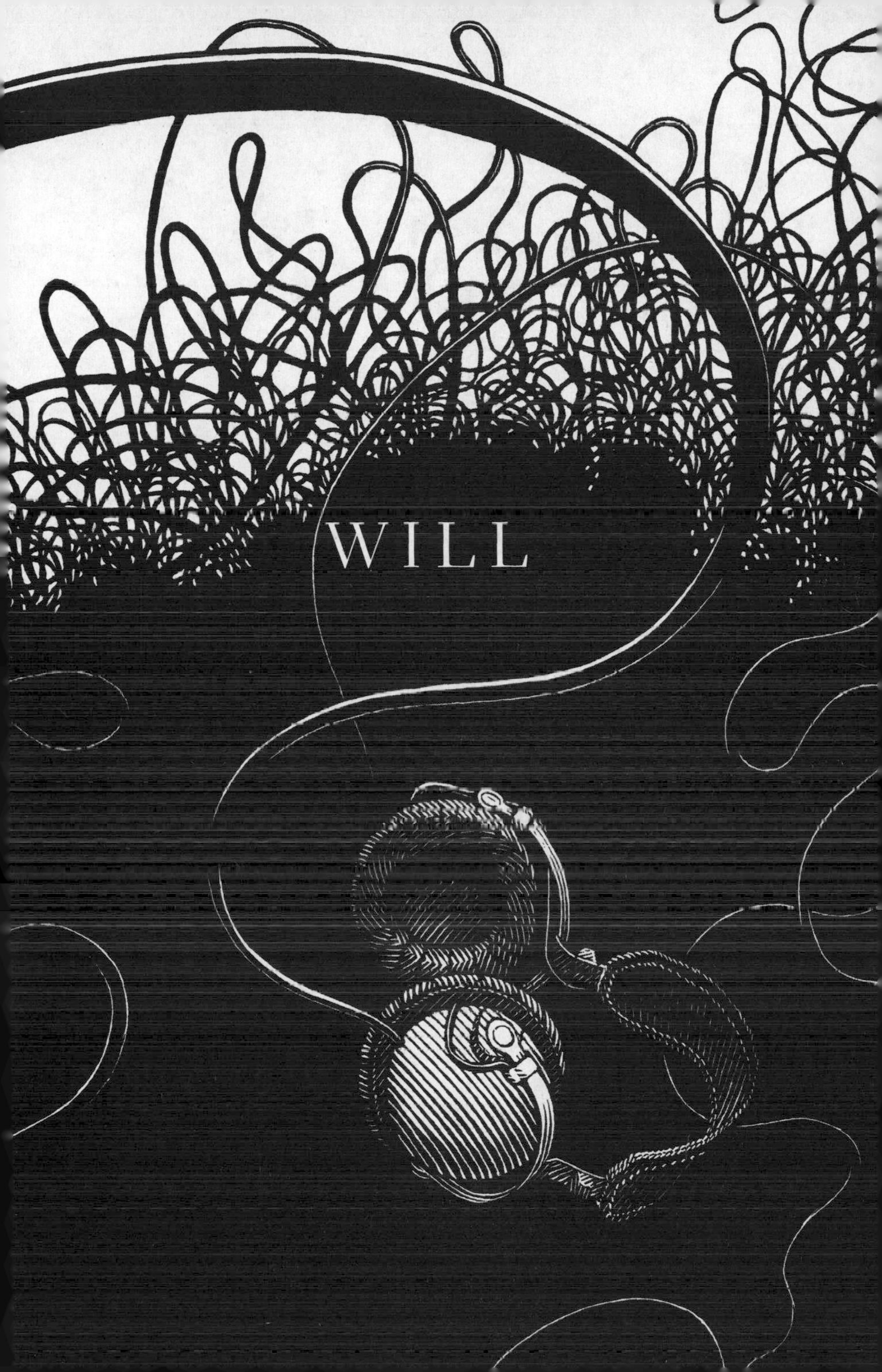

WILL

In hindsight, the thing that bothered me the most when I discovered what was happening to me was how blind I'd been. I'd seen what I wanted to see, something far removed from the truth.

Everyone else was being cured in a room, and the bomb shelter was certainly that. Everyone else had put something on their heads that was connected to wires or tubes or both. I had been given the headphones, big and weighty, and I had put them on willingly. The connections from the helmets went into the walls or the ceilings of their rooms; mine traveled into the wall of the bomb shelter. They'd all been underground, where no one could hear them screaming, which is exactly where I was.

It was difficult to accept the fact that Mrs. Goring and Rainsford had known all along. They'd known where I was and understood what I was doing. That was clear from the very start of my cure, which would reveal itself on not one but all seven monitors in the bomb shelter. Everyone else had endured the helmet with its screen and its sounds; I had the monkey phones and the monitors.

Rainsford's face appeared first in the center monitor, close and terrifying. I had suffered no contact with him other than a distant camera view; and there he was, near and personal. I hadn't expected to fear him as much as I did.

"I'm sorry, Will Besting," he began. "Really I am. But every treatment is different. Yours required a lot of preplanning and coordination. Unprecedented. It is, in the end, one of my many masterpieces."

I wasn't completely under his spell just yet, and inside, I was appalled by his arrogance. I wasn't a kid in trouble; I was a bug pinned to a wall, an experiment or a project, something to be achieved.

"Don't worry," he said, slowly and slithery, or was I starting to come undone? "You don't have to sell your soul; I'm already in you."

I wanted to grab the monkey phones and rip them off of my head, but it was like being hypnotized on a stage with a thousand people watching. At least that's what I'd heard from my mom, who had done just that in her twenties.

It was so bizarre. I knew what I was doing, but I couldn't stop.

She'd been acting like a chicken, clucking around the stage with a bunch of other idiots.

Strangest thing in the world, knowing something is all wrong but feeling that it's all right.

I felt all wrong, as my mother had.

What I *knew*: the headphones had to come off, and I had to run from thc room. But listening to Rainsford's voice, watching his wrinkled face in the center monitor, what I felt was not the same. *Leave the headphones on. Stand here. Watch. Take your medicine.*

Will Besting, 15

Acute fear: Peers, groups, crowds

"Most people forget, but not you, Will. You will remember. I'll see to it. Enjoy it while it lasts, Will Besting. Soon this will all be gone, wiped away, as if it never was. And with it, your fear."

He was sitting in the same chair that Ben Dugan had sat in, staring at me from the room in the boys' quarters with the numbers stenciled on the wall behind him. The *1* was gone—Ben's *1*—and the 3 and 4. All of them, gone. Only one number remained on the boy's wall: the number 6.

"It's time, Will," he said, taking a paintbrush in his hand and holding it where I could see. He dipped it in violet paint and stood, went to the wall, and blotted out my number.

What happened after that is not completely clear in my mind. Everything I saw was presented in flashing moments on all the screens; but I remember it as a single event, smashed into one endless space.

I'm sorry, Will.

There were many voices, but no faces, and I was walking. Everything was from my point of view, and it looked as if I was parting a sea of people. So many legs and dangling arms, standing so very close to me, all of them dressed in black or nearly black.

Many of the voices seemed to be talking about me as I passed through the throng, but they didn't know how well I could hear. They didn't know that hearing was my thing, that I listened better than most.

What's he going to do? He won't make it. He's fragile, always has been.

I saw my own line on the center monitor begin to rise in the bomb shelter, then stop, spreading out. A deep violet splotch of color bloomed at the bottom of the screen.

How did it happen? Did he have anything to do with it? No, no, that's not what happened. It was no one's fault.

All at once, I broke free of the oppressive bodies around me; but there were faces all around, ghastly and close up in every monitor, all pale with regret.

Oh, Will.

I don't know what to say.

Don't look. It will only hurt more.

No, do; it's what you need. It will help.

The violet splotch at the bottom of the screen spread like honey in the bomb shelter, filling half of the space.

I was standing alone now, looking down at a white-shirted figure lying in a box, my eyes trained perfectly on a button that hadn't been pulled through the buttonhole on the shirt. I reached out and fixed the clear button, patted the shirt down so it was nice and neat. It was a pressed shirt he wore, and the clear buttons looked so nice that I lingered there a moment.

What's he doing?

Why doesn't he move?

Someone go get the boy.

My eyes moved along the perfectly pressed shirt, and then I was looking at a chest, and then a neck. I saw the color first from the corner of my eye, like a blinding light. His bright green baseball cap, firmly pulled down low on his smooth forehead. It struck me as odd—my brother lying down in the box, wearing the pressed shirt and the green cap he never took off.

Why's he in the box? I asked.

Why's my little brother in the box?

For the smallest part of a second, I knew the truth, and then my whole world collapsed around me. Something deep inside split apart—what I saw and what would become my reality—and I ran from the coffin. A mob of people pushed and pulled, and I couldn't breathe. I had to get out. I had to run and never come back.

But the people wouldn't let me go. They were

everywhere. I fell, gasping for air, surrounded by pale and weeping faces.

The center screen in the bomb shelter filled with deep violet color. I felt a searing pain behind both ears, a scorching sting as if I had been cut by two knives, and then I was having a seizure. Was I on the floor in a funeral home surrounded by people who wouldn't let me escape, or was I in the bomb shelter with some part of me being sucked away, exchanged for something else?

I felt a piece of me return, the part I'd blotted out about Keith, a darkness I couldn't hold without losing my mind. Stillness then—a drifting through time—and then nothing. No feeling at all, just empty space.

When I awoke, the headphones were gone. I didn't take notice of this fact at first, nor the fact that the room itself had been greatly altered. The monitors, gone, replaced by a plain white wall. My backpack, gone, and with it my Recorder and my watch. The cot remained, on which I found myself lying.

All of these details eluded me on waking, because there was only room in my small world for one thought.

It was a thought so big that it could never fit in before; but now, on the other side of Rainsford's inhuman treatment, I could finally hold it inside and live with it.

My little brother wasn't alive. My Keith, with the stupid green baseball cap and the mad basketball skills. He'd been gone awhile—two years or more—and I felt the strangest, most unexpected thing at the sudden arrival of this information.

I was finally ready to let him go.

I cried, pretty hard, I think, the memories pouring out and away. The air hockey elbow shot in the basement that never worked; the way he moved in the driveway, slipping past me and driving to the hoop over our dented garage door. His inability to master the simple mechanics of running away from a robot, making me laugh until my sides ached.

It all melted into something soft and deep, a pain I could hold without falling apart.

You were a good little bro, Keith. The best.

You weren't too bad yourself.

His voice was never the same after that, which sort of broke my heart and kind of didn't.

Peace, bro. Peace wherever you are. See you on the other side.

The changed nature of the bomb shelter remained a secondary piece of information as I stood and wiped my eyes. There were two other things crowding my mind now, and they seemed of equal importance. Keith was not replaced but rather centered in the deepest part of my heart, where I knew beyond any doubt he would always stay.

My mind moved past Keith now and crept toward the first of two things: Marisa. So much had happened so very quickly, but now my thoughts swung back to her. We held the death of a close family member in common, us two, which made me want to go to her more than I ever had before. I knew her pain. And then, the biggest question of all: had she been cured?

The idea of the cure was what brought my own circumstance screaming back to the second thing that held my attention: was *I* cured? Like the others before me who had been so sure, I suddenly felt sure, too. Maybe it was knowing that Keith was with me, not some fake one

I was creating in the empty space around him. Or more likely, it had something to do with what had happened at the end of the cure. I felt the small space behind my ears. There were bones there, and tender skin below. And something new: small wounds, tender to the touch.

Those monkey phones did something to me. Something I was not supposed to know about.

I recalled what Rainsford had said: *Most people forget, but not you, Will. You will remember. I'll see to it. Enjoy it while it lasts, Will Besting. Soon this will all be gone, wiped away, as if it never was. And with it, your fear.*

There would come a time, soon it sounded like, when everything I knew about Fort Eden would vanish from my memory. *As if it never was.*

I had to find a way to make sure that didn't happen.

At last my mind had arrived at the reality of the moment. I felt battered and bruised, like I'd walked through a minefield and managed to live through three violent explosions.

"This can't be right," I said, staring at the bomb

shelter wall. When I said the words, I felt the fourth and final explosion ripping through my mind. It had been so numbingly quiet in the bomb shelter, the thought hadn't even occurred to me. Everything had seemed normal, but it wasn't. I said three more words, but they registered as a thought, not as sounds.

I can't hear.

Everyone suffered symptoms after the treatment, but no one had totally lost something in the exchange. It had been small things—a headache or a sleeping foot—but never an entire category of who they were. The idea of never hearing again struck me as the cruelest deception.

I yelled, not a word but a sound, and found that I had been wrong. The word sounded far away; but it was there, distant and weak. I yelled again, moving my jaw up and down like I'd dove too deep into a swimming pool and only needed to pop my eardrums. Was it better or the same? I picked up the edge of the rusted metal cot and dropped it on the concrete. The sound bounced quietly into my head and seemed to bring things closer.

"Can you hear me, Will?" I asked myself, loud but not yelling; and I heard my own voice. It was still small and far away, but my ears were getting better. It seemed, strangely, like the more I heard, the better I heard.

"This is what he meant," I said, too quietly to hear myself say it, but understanding perfectly. Rainsford knew that I'd lost my hearing, and he knew what this would mean: that I wouldn't hear him talking to me when I joined the rest.

"It's his voice; that's what makes them forget. It's what makes them do what he says."

But he'd also known that my hearing would return, at least most of it would; and when it did, his voice would undo my memory, break it apart, scatter it in the woods where I'd never find it again. I couldn't know this for sure, but all the evidence pointed to his powers of persuasion. And it seemed to me that his most powerful tool was his voice, a voice that lulled those around him into doing what he asked. Even if I was wrong, I decided not to take any chances. If hearing Rainsford would erase my memory, then I'd have to make sure and never hear his voice.

I looked once more at the bomb shelter and really took it in this time. Had there ever been a wall of monitors? I didn't have a watch anymore, and there were no windows in the basement. For all I knew I'd been in a deep sleep for days and days while they removed the monitors. The books were gone, too, and the monkey phones. Actually, the more I examined things, the more it seemed that *everything* was gone. Only the cot remained against one wall, on which I'd been sleeping.

I felt a gnawing hunger in my belly, and salivated at the thought of Mrs. Goring's canned peaches with the cinnamon thrown in.

Some food, that's what I need, and then I'll figure out what to do.

It wouldn't matter anymore if Mrs. Goring discovered she was missing a jar of preserves. She knew I was down here and had to imagine I was starving. I opened the door and stepped out. It wasn't as dark as I'd expected it would be in the basement. There was a soft, yellow light overhead, which hadn't been there before.

Outside the room I saw the wall of twisting mushrooms and, turning, the black door with the number 7.

"I'm not in the bomb shelter anymore," I said, hearing my words as if they were whispered from the end of a long hallway. "I'm at the bottom of Fort Eden. I'm in room number six."

It took me a few minutes to calm down and get past the idea that I'd been moved from one basement to another. The bomb shelter was real; I just wasn't in it. I stood before the door marked with a 7 and wished I'd had the courage to knock on it, but I didn't. It was the last room, *his* room. The only person who was going in there was Avery Varone, the girl who claimed she couldn't be cured.

I walked to the elevator, which stood open, and stepped inside. I took the long, slow ride up to the main floor. Staring at Kino's smashed canoe, I felt his life going in reverse and imagined him making different choices. When I got out, I walked up the ramp and Kino got bigger on the floor. Parting the curtain was the easy part; but standing at the door to Fort Eden, I had a familiar feeling. I was afraid. It wasn't the old, debilitating fear that grabbed me, but a new one, a rational one. I wasn't afraid of being with a bunch of people; I was afraid of what Rainsford would do to me if I went inside.

The door opened before I could turn around and go back.

"Get in here; I don't have all day, and the food's getting cold." Mrs. Goring, yelling in my face, loud enough for me to hear.

I stepped inside, nodding, and saw that everyone was sitting at the round table staring at me. In the past, this would have been my signal to cut and run, but I saw them differently than how I'd seen groups of people for a long time. They were smiling at me, saying things I couldn't hear. Even Connor was glad to see me, pumping his fist and, I think, even a little jealous that I'd put one over on the system, at least for a while.

Nice shirt!

I didn't hear Ben Dugan say the words; but he was pointing to his own, and I could read his lips. I looked down and saw that I had on the same one, the one with the *E* sitting on a blooming pedestal of stone.

I hadn't moved from the door, and Mrs. Goring was already back at her metal cart, which sat next to the table. She was moving big bowls of steaming pasta and sauce, and rolls of bread wrapped up in foil. A spaghetti dinner, my favorite. Alex and Kate were waving me over, calling my name, but I still didn't move.

When Marisa got up and started walking toward me, I met her halfway. She reached out her hand, smiling so perfectly, and our fingers touched. Her hand was shaking as much as mine was; and dragging me to the table, she kept looking back, wordless and beaming.

You're okay, I said, so softly that I heard nothing. She nodded as we arrived at the table, and I sat down. Her eyes looked tired, like she hadn't slept for days; and it worried me. Maybe she hadn't been cured after all.

"Eat. Now!" Mrs. Goring yelled from behind me. "I'll be back in twenty minutes."

Questions were firing left and right, and I caught the general idea: where have you been? Tell us everything.

I pointed to my ears, offered a start: "The cure left me just about deaf, but I can hear a little. I think it's coming back. Am I yelling?"

Friendly laughter followed, along with a lot of head nodding. *Dude, you're practically screaming at us*.

Food was making the rounds, the first real dinner I'd been this close to in a while, and I whispered close to Marisa's ear.

"Can you say something quiet and near? I want to hear your voice."

She smiled down at her plate, touched my hand under the table, and put her mouth next to my ear. If the hand holding had been amazing, this was completely off the charts. I felt her warm breath on my skin. The words were alive in my ear, and I heard them.

"Don't leave me again. Stay."

"No problem," I said, and everyone laughed. I had the feeling I'd said it pretty loud, and laughed along with them. I piled pasta onto my plate and covered it in thick, red sauce, then crunched my teeth into the best garlic bread I'd ever tasted. Things were looking up, no doubt.

As I scanned the table, I realized that Avery Varone wasn't there. I leaned in close to Marisa and asked where she was. She shrugged, pointing her fork toward the door leading outside, smiling absently. She was trying to put up a good front, but there was no mistaking how exhausted she was.

"Where's Rainsford?" I asked, and got the feeling I'd finally found the right volume for my voice.

Connor had the biggest voice in the group, but Kate was a close second, so I'd aimed my question at them.

"He's around," Kate said. "He says we're going home tomorrow."

"I'm actually going to miss this place," Alex Hersch offered. I heard his voice, quiet but there. My hearing was slowly getting better, and I understood the reason for the dinner. Rainsford knew that hearing voices would bring me back around. What better place to get people talking than around a dinner table?

I was starving and wanted nothing more than to eat everything in front of me, but I was smart enough to know it was a trick. The longer I stayed, the more I'd hear; and that, I knew, was dangerous.

"Can we take a walk? Is that allowed?" I asked Marisa.

She hesitated, not like she wasn't sure if they were allowed, but for a totally different reason. She was too tired to go for a walk.

"Go on," said Ben Dugan. "I'll hide some food for you. She'll never know."

This seemed to give Marisa just enough energy to get up and push me toward the door. The smile was back and we were moving. I looked over my shoulder, and was happy to see Ben taking my heaping plate into the guys' quarters.

I did take one slice of garlic bread with me, not for myself, but for Marisa. If the walk ended in a kiss, I wanted her to have the same breath I did. We held hands and walked the path to the pond, taking turns biting into the crisp bread until it was gone.

She leaned in close, putting her shoulder against mine. "You're cured," she said. "I'm happy for you."

"I'm happy for you, too," I said.

"You're yelling."

"Oh, sorry."

She smiled and looked at her shoes.

"Do you remember getting cured?" I asked, softer this time.

She shook her head no.

"But I'm not scared anymore. And I've put some things behind me. Hard things."

I wanted to say "I know," but I couldn't bring myself to do it. There would be time, later, to dig deeper into both of our pasts.

"Why so tired? Up late last night?"

She laughed, and the whisper was back, close and warm.

"Quite the opposite. I sleep all the time. Must be my symptom, like Kate's headaches and your hearing. Rainsford says it will go away after a while."

Maybe you're finally catching up on your rest, I thought, which felt true.

We fell into silence on the path, and I wished I had my Recorder. I'd have put one earbud in her ear, the other in mine, and played our song. It would have been epic-unforgettable-romantic-awesomeness. I was lost in this thought, thinking of the words and the tune, when she stopped me and looked into my eyes.

"You're singing our song," she said, softly enough so that I couldn't hear her; but I could tell what she'd said. And I realized that I was.

She leaned in, rising on her toes to meet me, and we kissed.

AVERY

When we arrived at the pond, Avery Varone was sitting alone on the dock. She was staring at the pump house, holding the pipe wrench in her hand.

Marisa touched me on the shoulder, signaling me to wait at the water's edge, and then she went to Avery's side and sat down. I couldn't hear what they were saying, but whatever it was, it wasn't much. Avery wasn't in a talkative mood. She kept glancing over at me, and I wondered again: *are you with us or against us?* She had overtaken Kate as the most likely mole in our group for a number of reasons.

I stared off at the pond, silence enveloping me, and thought about what I knew.

Kate Hollander was beautiful and smart, and she knew how to play people; but she wasn't a follower. Kate led. It was in her bones. I found it gradually harder to believe she would fall into step with someone else's plan, especially if it was a plan put into play by adults. She was classic antiauthority. She'd be the one at school pulling pranks and causing trouble for all the right reasons. I had come to trust Kate's motives in the days at Fort Eden, in part because I knew her tragic past, but also because she was a rebel fighting for us, not them.

So Kate was out, and Marisa wasn't even on the radar, which left only one person: Avery Varone. She was a foster kid, and I knew from her audio sessions that she'd been in at least nine different homes over the past few years. That sort of thing didn't happen if you were a good kid. My guess is that foster parents are in it for the money, and problem kids get moved along. But more than that was the central problem with Avery: she couldn't be cured, or at least that was her story. And standing by the pond that night, I thought I'd figured out why. Avery Varone couldn't be cured because she wasn't sick to begin with. It was the only answer that made any sense.

I was thoroughly convinced of these facts as Marisa got up and came back toward me, which made what she said all the more confusing.

"How's she doing?" I asked, making sure to whisper so my voice didn't carry over the dock. I moved closer so Marisa could answer me.

"Davis came back and saw her. She told him first."

"Told him what?"

Marisa looked hollowed-out with tiredness, as if she was walking in her sleep. Her words were faint, but clear enough.

"Avery's ready. She's going to do it. She's getting cured."

When we got back to the main room in Fort Eden, Marisa curled up on one of the couches and fell fast asleep. The guys were hustling one another at cards and tried to rope me in, but I waved them off and headed for the guys' room for at least three reasons.

1) I wanted the food Ben had taken for me.
2) I wanted to talk to Dr. Stevens.
3) I could hear them.

The third reason was the biggest. My hearing was rapidly returning. I was back to something like 50 percent, which was probably enough to hear Rainsford's voice or the haunting sound of garbled whispers if they returned.

I knew which bed was mine because my backpack had appeared on top of it. I searched under the bed and found the plate of food, set it on my lap, and stuffed a king-size wad of cold spaghetti into my mouth. I'd moved my backpack to the floor and unzipped the main compartment, then started digging. No Recorder. It was gone, as I'd suspected it would be. All the audio files, all the photos and videos of things that happened in the rooms. All of it gone.

"Hey, Will." Alex Hersch had entered the room from behind me. "We need a fourth for some cards. Come on; you can bring your food. Just stash it if Ms. Goring shows up."

"Give me ten, okay? I need to talk to Dr. Stevens real quick."

From outside the door, all the way at the table, I heard Connor Bloom calling my name.

"Come on, Will. Get your skinny ass out here! We got cards to play."

"I'll stall 'em," said Alex. "Just hurry up, okay?"

I nodded, forking another monster-size mouthful of spaghetti into my mouth. Three more bites and half a bottle of water from my backpack later, I was up and heading for the back of the room. There were two doors: a bathroom, which I peeked into and found expectedly trashed by three guys, and the room where the guys could sit and talk to Dr. Stevens. I went inside and saw the splotches of paint on the back wall. No more *1*, *3*, *4*, or *6*. All of them, including my own, were gone.

I sat in the chair and wondered if Mrs. Goring was in the bomb shelter watching me while she devoured her own plate of spaghetti.

There was a red button in front of the monitor, and I pushed it. Dr. Stevens came up on the screen about ten seconds later, as if she had been sitting there, waiting for my call, wondering why it had taken so long for me to show up. She smiled that slightly crooked smile of hers, sipped from a white coffee cup with a yellow smiley face on it. She sat behind her desk in her office.

The webcam was pointed at her face in a way that made her look slightly out of proportion.

"I'm so glad you're okay, Will," she said.

"Me, too."

"Are you mad?"

"What do you think?"

"You're mad."

"Dr. Stevens, I don't know what I am."

"You're cured," she said. "Don't underestimate how hard it was to pull that off."

"You lied to us."

"You won't feel the same in the morning. Trust me once more, okay? Everything is going to be fine."

"Why don't I believe you?"

"I don't know, but you should. You should believe me."

"How do you know Rainsford?"

"He was my mentor; I told you that. He's brilliant."

"How come he lives at the bottom of such a long staircase?"

She paused, thinking up a lie or a cover.

"Listen, Will. We took risks with you. New risks. You required an isolated connection to the group, something that would slowly draw you out. Just promise me you won't run off again. Stay put and listen to everything Rainsford tells you. Do that, and I absolutely promise that tomorrow morning you're going to feel a whole lot better about all of this."

"Good-bye, Dr. Stevens."

I didn't wait for her to say good-bye. I'd been looking at the cans on the floor and the brushes caked with dried paint. I picked up one, dunked it once in every one of the cans, all of which had begun crusting over at the top. By the time I was done, the brush was sopping with a gray goo that dripped onto the table and the floor. I swiped it across the computer screen, blotting out Dr. Stevens's face, and left the room.

I stopped at my backpack and searched inside one more time, dumping everything out on the bed. My clothes were there, and the Clif Bars and old wrappers. There were six water bottles, five of them empty. I searched the side pockets, unzipping them all until I came to the smallest one and felt something inside. Unzipping it, I discovered Keith's tiny MP3 player. I had put the player inside and had written the note, not Keith; and my long neurosis made my face flush with humiliation. I'd been getting pretty far out there before the cure, I realized, and in that respect I was okay with what Fort Eden had done to me.

My black earbuds were attached to the player, which I thought strange until I dug down into the pocket and found a Post-it Note. Not the one I'd written, but a new one. Someone else had written four words on the Post-it Note in block letters. They were four words I wasn't able to blot out of my mind for the rest of my time at Fort Eden.

DON'T LISTEN TO HIM

Whoever had taken the backpack had removed my Recorder, and with it every shred of evidence I had about this place. But they'd left the useless MP3 player, which couldn't record or take pictures; and someone had left the note.

Davis, I thought. *Had* to be Davis. He was there, trying to help me. He knew! The only thing now was to put in the earbuds and keep the music playing.

"Detroit Rock City," don't fail me now, I thought, dropping the MP3 player into my back pocket and running

the black wire up the spine of my T-shirt and pulling on my hoodie.

"Dude, Avery's getting cured, come on!"

I spun around, sure I was caught, and saw that Connor Bloom was coming toward me.

"Rainsford's on his way; we gotta get a move on. Cards will have to wait."

"Okay, yeah, I'm on my way."

But Connor Bloom was having none of it. He was behind me, pushing me toward the door, and he was easily twice as strong as I was.

"What's with the hoodie?" he asked me.

"Got a chill, I think I might have caught something out there in the woods."

"Don't cough on me. Football starts in a week."

We passed through the door, and I saw Marisa sitting up on the couch. She was rubbing her eyes and patting down her hair, which had gone wild on one side.

"Boy, I really zonked out, didn't I?" she asked no one in particular.

I looked at the opening where the stairs came up from the basement and saw shadows moving. As Rainsford came into view, it looked like he was rising out of the earth on a starless night. He was winded, but only slightly, and I got the feeling he'd taken his time climbing out of the gloom.

"Everyone, let's gather around," he said at length. He went to the round table and put out his arms as if to draw us in. "It's time we came to the end."

Rainsford looked at me, or through me, as Marisa arrived at my side and leaned on my shoulder. I couldn't see her with my hood pulled up, but she felt soft at my side, the warmth of sleep still lingering on her skin.

"Nice hat," she said. They would be the last words I heard her say until the next day.

"How are you feeling, Will Besting?" Rainsford asked me. "Can you hear me?"

"I can."

He nodded as if he thought this was excellent news.

"I'm glad to finally meet you."

And then the whispering started.

On their own, the sounds of Rainsford's voice and the whispering mass were hypnotic, but together their power was complete. They created a kind of acoustic dance I'd never heard before and never have since. The whispers turned soft and elastic, bouncing around Rainsford's voice like they were trying to get inside. Too, there was something tragic about the incomprehensible language below Rainsford's voice. It sounded, I thought, like the distant call of lost souls searching for a place to rest.

I struggled to keep my mind focused on a simple, imperative task: *get the music playing before it's too late.*

As everyone bustled to get around the table, I was able to secretly put the small earbuds in, place my hand in my back pocket, and hit PLAY.

Let's get this party started, I imagined Keith saying; and it was okay, a nice reminder that he was still tucked away in a place where I could always find him. I spun the dial in my pocket, turning the volume to about halfway, knowing that if I pushed it too far, Rainsford would hear the tinny sound of Kiss trying to shred my eardrums.

Avery was talking, and I wished I could hear what she was saying. She was finally telling everyone what she'd never told Dr. Stevens in all those sessions. She was telling her deepest fear. At the time I substituted the following: *Avery Varone, you are mortally afraid of the seventh room because that's where the monster lives. You do not want to go down there.*

I would later discover her true fear and roll it around in my head for weeks, trying to figure out the mystery of what could possibly cure her. I understood then why Avery believed she couldn't be cured. We all did. We understood, because she was afraid of the biggest thing of all: death.

Avery Varone was terrified of dying.

I thought then as I do now that Rainsford had met his match. In order for Avery to be cured, she would have to experience her fear. She could only find relief on the other side of the grave, because in Rainsford's world, dying was the only cure for someone like Avery. He would have to kill her, and that wouldn't be a cure at all but rather the culmination of a long nightmare.

And yet the proceedings continued. I watched as Rainsford's eyes passed over each person, including me. I watched as he got up and left the table, looking back just once as he started down the long, winding stairs. I put my hand in my back pocket, dialed the music down very slowly, and found that the room was quiet.

"You can do it, Avery. It's going to be fine," Kate was saying as she touched her on the forearm.

"I know. I'm ready. This is going to work."

Alex, Connor, and Ben got up as one and wandered

aimlessly toward the guys' dorm as the girls gathered around Avery. It felt like my cue to leave, so I got up, too, touching Marisa on the small of her back. I wanted to ask everyone if they really thought this was a good idea, but I was afraid of what that might mean. If I disagreed or questioned what was happening, they'd know something wasn't right.

At the time, I didn't know what Avery's fear was; but even if I had known, I'm not sure I would have had the courage to try and stop her. I moved to one of the couches, felt the guilt wash over me, and stared at the gaping maw of stone teeth leading down to the seventh room.

A few minutes later Kate and Marisa went to their quarters and I was alone with Avery. She hadn't moved from the table.

"Are you sure this is what you want?" I asked. It was the best I could come up with, and it wasn't much.

She didn't answer me. Instead, she got up, walked directly to the winding stairs, and started her descent. I thought she was simply going to leave, but she turned at the very last second. She wasn't afraid; she wasn't anything—her expression was as blank as an empty piece of paper.

"Good-bye, Will."

She was gone, and I was alone in the main room of Fort Eden. There were answers down below, answers I wasn't sure I wanted to find. It would be nice, I thought, to be ignorant and cured like my friends. But I had a different fate than all the rest. I was meant to know. I would find the truth at the end of a winding stone stair, in the seventh room, at the very bottom of Fort Eden.

When the last of the light from above was gone, it felt as if I was walking toward a nightmare in progress. Not *in* the dream, but over it, feeling its force drawing me down. There came a stretch of steps in which there was no light at all, and I found myself stumbling on steps that felt less and less firm. They crumbled under my feet, like they were made not of stone, but of hard clay grown old and cracked. Some of the steps were completely torn away across the middle; and not being able to see them, I slid five or more feet in the pitch-black. When I came to a stop, a sliver of light appeared in the dust settling around me. The light was somewhere below, around one or more turns, and I knew that the moment to turn back was upon me.

This is it, Will, I told myself. *Either get it over with or start climbing. You'll never get up enough nerve to do this again.*

And so it was that I somehow found a well of courage I didn't think existed. I've never considered myself a brave person. It certainly wasn't a muscle I'd put much training into during the previous two years. But there it was, the will to go on and the desire to make myself do it.

I came to a landing where the stairs stopped. To one side, a large door was open just a crack—the source of the light that had drawn me down. Past the door the stairs continued. I went to the edge, where the winding way continued deeper still.

There was no noise from inside the room, and as I touched the door gently, it opened a few more inches. It was solid, with iron bolts and casings, and it made no sound on its hinges. I didn't have to go inside; I knew what was in there simply by the object I saw through the crack. That cup. The cup with the smiley face on it.

Dr. Stevens was there. She was at Fort Eden. She'd been there all along.

Trust me, Will, one more time.

I think I'll pass, if it's all the same to you, I thought.

I opened the door far enough to go inside but didn't. I saw bookshelves on the wall, a desk, a computer—very much like her office back in the city. Dr. Stevens wasn't sitting in her chair or standing behind the door with a baseball bat. She wasn't in the room, and I had a feeling I knew why. She'd be where Avery was. She'd be down, farther still. I left the door ajar as it was when I'd found it, light bathing the stairway, and then I kept on.

The last stretch of stairs was the hardest. There were peculiar noises down there of a kind I knew nothing about. If I had to guess, I would have said there were machines and liquid and power of some kind at work in the seventh room. They were the sounds of the other cures, only amplified and stretched into something worse. My hearing was getting to maybe 60 percent—no more. A scattered light crept up at my feet, but it was swallowed by the dark. The stairs, the walls, the ceiling—they'd all turned black and dull while I wasn't paying attention. The walls around me seemed to consume light, to absorb it. One more step and I could lean around a sharp corner and see.

I heard faraway voices and knew who they belonged to.

Dr. Stevens: *Thirty seconds and we're there.*

Then Mrs. Goring, her unmistakable gravelly voice echoing off the walls:

Don't be so sure. She might not even make it.

She'll make it.

Without knowing I was doing it, I'd let my head slip around the last, sharp corner. It was a miracle I didn't gasp, or maybe I did and they just couldn't hear me. A six-sided room lay before me, each wall holding a monitor encased in stone. Ben's wall was brutally scrawled with dozens of blue number *1*s, like a madman had dunked his hand in a can of paint and slapped the numbers into place, drawing his hand down along the stone. On the monitor, Ben's cure replayed; but only the part where he was flooded with fear. Over and over, the small boy picked up the arm in the sandbox, his eyes going wide with fear as the spider crawled onto his hand. The sounds were stretched and pulled apart, as if someone was trying to extract something from them.

All six walls were like this: a monitor embedded in stone, repeating the most terrifying parts of each cure, surrounded by violently written numbers and colors that matched the patients.

Ben Dugan—Blue
Kate Hollander—Purple
Alex Hersch—Green
Connor Bloom—Orange
Marisa Sorrento—White
Will Besting—Violet

Cords and tubes ran out of the ceiling above each monitor. They came together in the middle like a canopy, where they were bunched together with a thick rope. From there, the whole wiry mass ran down a narrow hall to a room I could not see. It was from this hidden room that the voices echoed. It was a room I knew had a number like all the rest: number 7, where Avery Varone was getting cured or killed or both.

I'd made it that far only to find my courage failing me. What if they saw me come down the narrow hall? They'd know my memory was still intact. They'd chase me down and *make* me listen to Rainsford.

Voices echoed through the chamber once more as I managed to step around the corner and begin walking slowly.

Mrs. Goring: *It's not going to work. Pull it!*

Dr. Stevens: *No! Leave them alone! Just stay back!*

The hall was dark and slathered with painted number 7s, but at the end of the hall there was light and movement. Seconds later, after reluctantly forcing myself forward, I was able to peer around the last corner at the bottom of Fort Eden.

Avery Varone was sitting in a large chair, facing away from me. She had the helmet on, and the tubes and wires were running up into the ceiling. Sitting next to her, also facing away, was Rainsford. He, too, wore a helmet bursting with wires and tubes.

Say it's not true, I thought.

Dr. Stevens: *She's flooding. Do it now!*

Mrs. Goring: *I won't!*

Dr. Stevens pushed Mrs. Goring aside and threw a lever on the wall. I watched helplessly as both Rainsford and Avery went rigid and the wires and tubes went wild overhead.

Say it's not true, I thought again.

The two of them were connected. Something was passing between Rainsford and Avery Varone. Understanding this fact produced reasonable questions I didn't want to ask.

Had I been attached to Rainsford when I was cured? Were all of us? And the biggest question of all: *WHY?*

It was over swiftly, and with it, all sound died. Stillness at the bottom of the world, and then words.

Mrs. Goring: *She's dead.*

Dr. Stevens: *She's not.*

Mrs. Goring: *She is.*

Dr. Stevens: *Just give her a second. She'll be fine.*

For the first time since I'd met her, Mrs. Goring seemed the slightest bit sad. When she spoke again, the edge in her voice had returned, and I thought that this was my best chance to get away. While she was talking I backed up, but I heard enough. Enough to know that I should never have trusted Dr. Stevens.

Mrs. Goring: *You went too far.*

Dr. Stevens: *I'm his daughter. I did what I had to do.*

Mrs. Goring: *You're wrong. No one forced you.*

Dr. Stevens: *Shut up.*

Mrs. Goring: *Her blood is on your hands.*

Dr. Stevens: *I said shut up!*

I had a lot of questions as I took two stairs at a time, escaping from the seventh room before they could see me. *Was Avery still alive? What had really happened during all of our cures? What had I just witnessed?* But I had one answer I knew for sure, and it made me feel scared for every one of us.

Rainsford had a daughter, and her name was Dr. Stevens.

That night no one came out of the rooms. There was no greeting for Avery, because Avery didn't come back. I crept into my bed and lay there, staring at the ceiling, for a long time. The battery on the MP3 player had maybe an hour left, and I kept the earbuds in and my hoodie pulled up just in case. About midnight I got up and peeked into the main room, which was empty and eerily quiet. I tiptoed across to the girls' quarters and went inside.

Two empty beds, two full ones. The thought of accidentally waking Kate instead of Marisa weighed heavy on my mind as I stood at the door. Either way, both girls were conked out solid, and I couldn't see the point of waking Marisa. What could I say? If she had been controlled in a way that made her forget, nothing I said was going to do any good. It would all sound insane, and might even put her and the others in needless danger. I went back to my bed and vowed to keep my mouth shut until morning.

A person entered the guys' quarters some time later. I'd been drifting in and out of sleep with my finger on the PLAY button. The door opened and closed, and then the garbled whispering began and I turned on the music, rolling over on my bed so the hoodie flopped over my face. The intruder had to be Rainsford, and he walked back and forth between the beds saying who knew what. I couldn't hear him, but Connor, Ben, and Alex could. Their dreams were filled with Rainsford telling them what to remember about this place.

After a while he left and I heard him enter the girls' quarters. I turned off the music, but the searching whispers remained. I had maybe a half hour of juice left, nothing more, and I let the music play through Kiss and The Who, the Rolling Stones and Led Zeppelin.

By the time the music died I was fast asleep.

Morning at Fort Eden came early. Mrs. Goring was in the main room, banging two frying pans together, and she was in the nastiest mood I'd ever seen.

"Get up and get out!" she yelled. There was no formal breakfast served, no warm good-bye from the mysterious proprietor, nothing. She stuck a granola bar and a bottle of water in each of our hands as we passed by and answered our questions as tersely as the human language would allow.

"Is Avery cured? Where is she?" Marisa asked. She was more awake than she'd been the day before, which pleased me.

"She's staying an extra day," Mrs. Goring said, shoving the meager breakfast in Marisa's hands.

"No way, *alone*?" Ben Dugan asked.

"Ben Dugan, you are a fool. Of course not alone! I'll be here."

"Super fun for Avery," Kate said under her breath.

"You I won't miss," Mrs. Goring countered.

"Where do we go?" asked Connor Bloom, who looked half asleep as he walked by and begged for an extra granola bar, which Mrs. Goring would not give him.

"Same place you came from, up the path. Your ride'll be waiting."

"Tell Rainsford thanks," Alex Hersch said, and I could tell by the sound of his voice that he really was thankful for having been cured. "If he needs another Davis, tell him I'll be first in line."

"I'm not telling him squat!" Mrs. Goring said.

When my turn came in the line, I waved off the granola bar but took the water. Everyone had gone outside, and it was just us two.

"Suit yourself," she said. "Like I care if you starve."

I was about to move through the doorway and out into the clearing when she grabbed me by the arm and held me back. She looked into my eyes, searching for something.

She knows, I thought. *She knows, and she's going to throw me down those stairs so my memories can be erased like the others.*

But then something unexpected happened. Her eyes began to fill with tears as she stared up at me. Her chin wobbled funny, like she was going to weep for some deep regret she didn't know how to explain. She let me go, leaned over the wobbly metal cart I had come to know so well, and took hold of a small brown box.

"You won't know what it means," she said, "but I have to tell someone, and you're all I've got." And for once I could imagine her as a young girl of my age, innocent and happy. There was that part of her, locked away; and it proved my point about the power of sound. In her voice was the girl she had once been, before life had disappointed her bitterly. She was not always mean Mrs.

Goring. She was once an innocent girl with fears and dreams.

I took the box and put it in my backpack, then I reached out and touched her on the arm, because it seemed like she needed someone to touch her in a kind way just then.

"Get on the path, Will Besting. There's a life out there. Go live it," she said, the old salt returning.

I wanted to tell her that I could probably make it back here for a visit if only I had a driver's license, but I let it pass.

On the long walk up the path, I stayed next to Marisa, and we talked about nothing special. My hearing was at around 70 percent, so I leaned in a lot when she spoke, which she seemed to like. I could hear the crows following us at a distance in the canopy above, as they'd done on the way in, cawing back and forth. Were they happy to see us leaving, or just annoyed at our presence in the thick of the woods?

"Does everyone still have symptoms?" I yelled ahead to the group that led.

The consensus was yes, everyone was still suffering from some strange ailment, and I began to wonder if we'd all left something at Fort Eden that we'd never get back.

Ben Dugan surprised everyone when he yelled Avery's name over our heads.

"Avery Varone! You're back!"

She was jogging up the path, trying to catch up to us as we stopped.

"Thank God," I mumbled, "she's okay." Deep inside I was thinking how great it was that Fort Eden wasn't a murder scene and that my life would not become hopelessly complicated after all. Avery Varone, not dead, meant a lot. It meant I could forget everything that I'd seen if I wanted to and it wouldn't matter. We were all cured, and no one was terribly hurt. As bizarre as the experience had been, at fifteen, I could imagine letting that be enough.

"So, are you better?" Kate asked. She'd come through the throng of people and met Avery first. She didn't wait for an answer while Avery caught her breath. "Yep, she's cured. A girl knows."

Avery nodded, smiling, and we all seemed to notice the change in her at once.

"Very goth of you," Kate commented, picking up a long strand of Avery's hair that we all saw had turned white.

"I know, right?" Avery said. "It'll grow out. No worries."

We talked a little more, but the white van awaited, and we all wanted to go home. Everyone pulled out their phones along the way, still finding no signal; and they all discovered that if they had taken any pictures, those pictures were gone. They didn't care about this detail as much as they should have, and I was convinced that this was all part of the plan. Get cured, go away, remember nothing.

When we'd climbed the entire path and the trees around us had fallen away, the morning had already turned warm. Sweatshirts were wrapped around waists and bottles of water were drained. Dr. Stevens and her white van were not there, so we waited, wondering what we were supposed to do.

A few minutes passed and then a sound came from up the washboard road. We saw the dust rising first, then the dirt bike. It wasn't Dr. Stevens in the white van, not yet.

"It's him," said Avery, smiling as she tucked the wiry white strands of hair behind her ear. "He came back, just like he said he would."

"Who did?" asked Ben Dugan.

"Davis," said Kate, a sliver of jealousy returning to her voice.

"Maybe he'll let me ride his bike," said Connor. "Should I ask him?"

"Not a great idea, bro," Alex confided, and I had to agree. Connor Bloom was still a little on the wobbly side. He'd stopped twice on the way up the trail, leaning hard against a tree. Putting him on a dirt bike seemed like a terrible idea.

A plume of dirt rose off the back of Davis's bike as he came near. He wore a white T-shirt, jeans, boots, and no helmet. He'd been cured, like the rest of us, so maybe he'd developed a fear of anything being placed on his head. Either way, the look suited him, and I was glad once more that he'd chosen Avery over Marisa from the start.

"So you guys are a wrap, huh?" he said, killing the engine as he arrived, and we all circled around a 500cc dirt bike that looked made for riding through the woods.

"Sweet ride," Connor said, nodding appreciatively.

"Don't let him near it," Kate warned. "He'll run us all over."

We laughed, and Davis smiled broadly. He didn't get off the bike, glancing around at the group. The sun was up over the road behind me, so when our eyes met, he squinted into the bright light.

"Good to see you, Will. Everything cool?"

The question was like a wink—Did you get the music I left for you? Do you remember? Did you figure anything out?—but it felt like the wrong time to give anything away. I needed to be free and clear of this place and get my head straight. It didn't matter though. Avery Varone was getting on the bike, which pulled everyone's attention away from me.

"Hey, if you're giving rides, count me in," Kate said, and I felt a little worried for Avery. Kate Hollander on the back of the bike with her arms and legs wrapped around Davis . . . well . . . not too many guys I know could experience that without thinking twice.

Avery shocked everyone with her reply.

"Tell the doc I'll meet you guys back in the city," she said. "I raced up here so fast I forgot to bring my bag."

"You want me to take you back?" Davis asked.

Avery's arms were already around his middle, her cheek resting on his white T-shirt.

"Here comes Dr. Stevens," I said, seeing the dust start to rise way up the long hill, the white van off in the distance.

"Go, Davis," Avery said; and looking at her, I saw that her eyes were closed. "Just go."

The engine fired and our circle parted. There was something very cool about the whole thing, and everyone began to cheer them on. But I had mixed emotions as Davis shrugged, smiled, and put the bike in gear.

"Enjoy being cured, you guys," he said, and they started down the path.

Marisa waved and hopped up and down.

"I can't believe he came back for her," she said, taking hold of my hand.

"God, it's like a lovefest around here," said Kate, the most popular girl somehow managing to end up alone at the end. Connor and Ben each put an arm around her as the van rolled up, and this seemed to bring her around.

I looked down the path, listening for the dirt bike. But it was already outside my range of hearing. Seeing them go down there, where the trees turned the path dark and shadowy, I was really glad for Avery Varone and thought again about how much I knew. I wondered if, later on, after I'd had time to think about it, I'd wish I could forget like everyone else.

Dr. Stevens was all smiles, excited to see everyone and especially curious about me. She searched my eyes, and when it appeared that I'd passed some sort of test, we all began piling into the van. She took the news of Avery's departure in stride.

"I've known Davis a long time," she said. "He'll get her home."

"Wherever home is *this* week," Kate said, getting in one last jab, but then apparently thinking twice. "Okay, that was beneath even me. Wipe it from your memories, folks."

"You're right, that was low," said Dr. Stevens, and then she let slip a piece of information I knew was more important than it seemed on the surface. "She's with me now. The last place didn't work out, and I decided ten homes was enough."

Dr. Stevens had become Avery's foster parent. *How convenient*, I thought. If Avery had died during her cure, Dr. Stevens probably would have had a way to make her disappear.

When I reached the backseat of the van, Marisa sat next to me. Ten minutes later she was sleeping with her head against my shoulder and we were out on the highway heading back into the city. I opened my backpack and searched inside, finding the small box Mrs. Goring had given me. It was tied shut with a piece of twine, which I untied and dropped into my bag.

Inside the box I found my Recorder and, cycling through the menu, discovered many files. All the audio files I'd taken from Dr. Stevens's office were there, plus every audio file I'd recorded at Fort Eden. All the photos I'd taken and all the videos I'd shot, all of them were there. And Mrs. Goring had added more things for me to listen to, more things to watch.

The conversation between Rainsford and Dr. Stevens rose up in my memory.

I'm not sure she can be trusted.

Don't be ridiculous. Of course she can. She'll play her part; I'll see to it.

It was not Avery or Kate or Marisa Dr. Stevens didn't trust. It was Mrs. Goring.

I looked up at Dr. Stevens, who was staring at me in the rearview mirror, and wondered what I was going to do.

You were right about her, I thought. *She's betrayed you.*

But what did that even mean?

I would discover, on that very night, the whole truth of the matter.

It was far worse than I'd imagined.

RAINSFORD

One Month Later

We asked you a question, Will. Why are you hiding in this room all alone?

Because I knew. I knew, and I was afraid.

I remember when I was in the bomb shelter all alone, I thought about what would happen if someone found me. I came up with that answer based solely on the idea that I was afraid of being with other people. It had nothing to do with Rainsford or what happened to us at Fort Eden. I was just too afraid to go inside and face my fear.

As it turned out, I never had to deliver that answer in the bomb shelter at Fort Eden; and, in the end, I'm not sure how I feel about that. If someone would have come looking for us and found me hiding there, everything about my life and the lives of the others would have been different. None of us would have been cured. We'd all still be mired in darkness, trying and failing to make ourselves well again. But we'd each paid a price, some bigger than others; and I knew things no person should be forced to know alone.

Connor Bloom still hasn't recovered from his dizzy spells, which has brought his athletic career to an end. Everyone is saying he was hit too hard one too many times as he carried the ball, but I know better.

Ben Dugan called me just this morning, and I asked him again, like I always do: how are your hands feeling? He says he's gotten used to it—the pain in his joints—that it's gotten a little better.

Kate still has the headache that won't go away.

Alex's feet fall asleep all the time, so he can't do driver's ed until they get it figured out.

I have fallen head over heels for Marisa, who is sleeping on the small couch in my room as I say these words into my Recorder. She sleeps a lot. She always will.

One month later, I know I'll never get all my hearing back. I've settled for 70 percent and hope it won't get worse. But it will. I'm nearly positive I'll be totally deaf by the time I'm thirty, but I hold out a little bit of hope.

I feel certain about the lasting nature of these ailments because Mrs. Goring explained a few things to me. She didn't just give me back my Recorder; she filled it with things I wish I hadn't discovered. It began with her voice, quieter than usual, and more human.

I've carried these secrets for sixty-two years, but the time has arrived for me to speak, and speak I will. Hear me, Will Besting. Hear me and know.

The first thing I would like to say is that he chose poorly. He should have known better. I might have been afraid, but I was not a pawn. It takes a certain kind of strength to sit in the seventh chair. I had the vigor for it. I could endure. But I was not the person he thought I was, and this has brought me to you, Will, at the twilight of my years.

Rainsford has been my husband these many years, and Dr. Stevens—or Cynthia, as I prefer to call her—is my daughter. As you are probably well aware by now, Cynthia is very attached to her father. She has done many bad things for him, although it's hard to say how much she really knows half of the time. You've seen the power Rainsford wields. My guess is, that power is amplified in Cynthia. She does as he says.

Cynthia gathered the seven. It was her primary purpose, at least so far as Rainsford was concerned. She was given the assignment without my knowledge—I want that known, so don't leave it out. Your arrival and the arrival of your friends was sudden. I had very little to do with the proceedings. It was the two of them mostly.

The hardest part of what I must tell you is easier to show you. There's also the simple matter that you won't believe me if I say it. Don't lose heart, Will Besting. I've taken you this far; you must go with me the rest of the way. You must come out of the dark where you hid in the hall. You can't turn back and run up those winding stairs this time. Now you will stay, come into the room, and see. Now you may open your eyes.

I knew what Mrs. Goring—she'll always be called that in my mind—was talking about. There was a file on my Recorder with a peculiar name, so I knew where to look. The file was in all caps: OPEN YOUR EYES. The file I just transcribed was called ME FIRST! I obeyed the command, and the commands put forth by some of the other file names. Others were AFTER YOU SEE and ME FOURTH! and so on. Mrs. Goring was not a subtle person. The instructions were loud and clear.

OPEN YOUR EYES was a video file I clicked on; and not wanting to miss anything important, I put on my headphones and cranked up the volume. The video showed Rainsford with the helmet on. He was in the seventh room where all had gone quiet. I was long gone, probably in the guys' quarters already, as Mrs. Goring zoomed in close on Rainsford. He was old, and whatever procedure had taken place, it looked as if it had killed him and he was already decaying before my eyes. But I could not have been more wrong. Dr. Stevens and Avery were gone, or so it seemed. It was only the old man and Mrs. Goring, the two of them alone beneath Fort Eden.

His face began to move oddly, as if it was liquid. His hair was disheveled and gray around the edges of the helmet. I blinked hard as the camera zoomed in even closer: only his face in the lens, the eyes closed and the corners of the mouth turned down. The wrinkles on his forehead began to peel away. His crow's feet, once deep and rutted, softened. His hair began to darken at the tips, and I felt a sting of recognition. The helmet lifted up off his head, pulled up to the ceiling by a chain. When he opened his eyes, they were a brilliant blue, but they were not the eyes of an old man.

It was Davis who sat in the chair. They were not two men, but one.

They were the same person.

I will admit to a morbid fascination with that video. I watched it four more times before continuing on, and each time I tried to find reasons why it couldn't be true. Rainsford and Davis had been in the same room at the same time, hadn't they? At first this felt true enough, but putting the question to the test, I couldn't say for sure. I'd thought Davis was helping me; wasn't that true? But it had been Mrs. Goring who'd given me the MP3 player and told me not to listen.

Another thought prevented me from watching the video for a sixth time: *Mrs. Goring was once young, like Avery. And so was Rainsford.*

ME FOURTH! began thus:

Now you know the most terrible part. The rest won't be

so bad, although there is the cure, which I admit has a ghastly quality. Let's give it a rest for a few seconds and talk about Rainsford while you recover your strength.

He has had many names, a new one every seventy-seven years. But I prefer to call him only Rainsford, and so I will.

Don't ask me to explain why the seventy-seventh year matters so much, because I don't know. And I beg you—don't waste your time trying to make Rainsford into a vampire. It's quite the opposite—without Rainsford, there is no vampire. If such a legend exists at all, he is him.

I grew old, but so did he. And I had no memory of what he'd done. My life before the cure has always been a blur, like a piece of glass smeared with paint. He could have gotten away with never telling me. It took a batch of strong moonshine to find the truth. Oh, how he liked to talk when I got him on the hooch.

If Rainsford is to be believed, I was his fifth wife. Do the math, Will Besting. Rainsford has been around for a long time.

The ME FIFTH! audio file began:

How he became the way he is, at the very start, is hard to say. I'm not sure even he knows. I know he was

connected to a great deal of money and status as a child, because he told me as much. The question, I suppose, would be, When exactly was he a child? And by that I mean truly an infant, not the third or fourth go-around. Whenever it was, money and power had roles to play. Someone spent a fortune figuring this out; and as far as I know, Rainsford was the only beneficiary.

Immortalist. *That's the best word I can think of to describe Rainsford. He has devised a way to live forever—or someone devised it for him long ago—and he chooses to keep doing it. I hesitate to mention this for fear it will come back and bite me, but I have tried to kill him. Twice, actually. Once when I was forty and again when I was sixty-seven. About every twenty-five years, give or take.*

The first time was after I learned the truth and he was passed out on the floor in the main room of our home, which you know as Fort Eden. I shot him through the heart with a pistol. Not a trace of blood; in fact, it woke him up. He sat bolt upright and asked me if I might be willing to make him some dinner, which I did. Twenty-five odd years later I hit him over the head with an iron rod, and he fell off the dock into the pond. He endured a period of years in which he hated going down there, but after that he knew what I'd done and things got ugly.

Was he unkillable? Is *he? Hard to say.*

His seventy-seventh year couldn't come fast enough, and that's when he and Cynthia began scheming behind my back. The proceedings had a certain rhythm to them, like it had all happened four or five times before. She did anything he asked; but he never told her the truth, and neither did I. How could I? She believed he was brilliant. She believed what she told you, that he was her mentor. That the process would cure both him and you. And I suppose, technically, she was right.

It's a shame I'll have to tell her he's dead. I can't think of what else I can come up with; and either way, he's gone. Rainsford won't show his face around here again until she and I are both in our graves.

Bastard.

ME SIXTH! was the last audio file she added to the Recorder. It begins here:

I turn now to the cure. If you're not sitting, I suggest you do so. This won't be easy.

Facing the worst of your fear in the room has little or nothing to do with making you well. People have been trying that stuff for a thousand years. For someone as screwed up as you, immersion therapy is a waste of time.

No, the flooding was for his benefit, not yours. It's his blood that cures you, and your blood that makes him young again. It has to happen during his seventy-seventh year. If he waits beyond that, some of his old blood starts to have real problems. Sooner, and the new blood has no effect. There must be something about the seventy-seventh year—like a flower blooming for a season—when the procedure works like it's meant to.

He requires seven transfusions from seven different subjects over no more than seven days. And they can't be just any transfusions. They have to be flooded, and acute fear is the safest way of getting it. Check behind your ears; you'll find two small scabs. The helmets and the headphones are alike that way—when you flood with fear, he digs in and takes what he needs. And he sends some of his blood in your direction, too. It's his blood that cures you. Forget all that fear-based garbage. You and your friends are well because you have a transfusion of immortalist blood in you. Not enough to make you live much longer than your normal life spans, but enough to cure what ails you.

The first six subjects turn him young again, but only for a little while—several hours or a day, depending on the person on the other end. Girls work better for some reason. The seventh is the most important—she's the one that makes it stick.

Before you start liking Rainsford for giving you some of his blood, you should know one thing: the blood he's giving you is the stuff he needs to get rid of. He has to get it out of his system and replace it with the fear-flooded blood you provide. It's why you're all old in one way or another; get it? You probably don't.

Ben Dugan's got arthritis, and he'll have it for the rest of his life.

Kate Hollander has a blood clot in her brain. Hopefully a stroke won't kill her, but it probably will.

Alex Hersch has circulation problems in his legs. One day they'll go to sleep and never wake up.

Connor Bloom has a bad case of senile dementia. He's as dumb as a dishwasher, so nobody is likely to notice; but the dizzy spells won't go away. He's stuck with those.

You like Marisa, and I hope it works out. Just know what you're getting yourself into. She's fatigued in general and always will be. She'll nap like a cat her whole life.

And you, Will Besting, you got a raw deal, too. Enjoy that hearing while you've got it, because it ain't gonna last much longer. I give you twenty years, tops.

Avery Varone got the white hair, which makes me hate her more than anything I can think of. It's what I got, too. It's the lottery in this situation. She'll be totally white-haired in another decade, but that's it. Otherwise she'll grow old just the same as Rainsford. He probably planned it that way, though I have no idea how.

I don't know, nor do I care, what you do with this information. My only debt was to say the words. Where the words go after I'm gone is not my problem. You strike me as a feeble young man. I'll be honest with you. If I could have chosen, I would have taken Kate Hollander in a second. Her I liked. She would have screamed the truth from the rooftops. But the circumstances surrounding your cure were what made my plan possible. Without them, the secrets of Fort Eden would be gone forever.

In the end, I know he'll erase my memories, too, and that will be the final insult. At least I won't have to remember his ugly face.

Do what you want, Will Besting. My obligation is met.

I can see her, and it makes me sad. She is alone, sitting on the dock, staring at the pond as winter settles in over the water. The trees are barren, and she is old. Her chosen one has betrayed her, left her to die alone in the coldness of the woods. She is not thinking about Avery as she stares at the water, this girl who completed the circle. She is not thinking of very much at all, because what she knew has been erased. Rainsford fixed the pump at the pond, so she'll have plenty of water. There are enough canned goods in the basement of the Bunker to last a lot longer than she will. Her fate is sealed; her time has passed.

Marisa awoke briefly just now, and we played Berzerk on my Atari 2600 for a half hour. Then we each put one earbud in an ear and listened to our song—*I Wanna Be Adored*—and she drifted back to sleep as we held hands.

If we're lucky and we stay together to the end, she'll sleep twenty hours a day and I'll stumble around the house, unable to hear a word she's saying. But it'll still be heaven. We won't be afraid, and my memory of these events will have faded. One day we'll find each other on the other side, healed and whole again. Keith and Marisa's dad will be there, and our friends and the rest of our families. Mrs. Goring will be waiting for us, and so will Avery Varone.

There is, of course, one person we won't find no matter how long we wait.

One day Avery Varone will sit on the dock at the pond alone. Her companion will be young again, but she will be old; and she, too, will be made to forget. She will perform the task that lies before her because he'll ask her to. And then she will be alone, and Rainsford will go on as he always does, as he always will.

The old Eden is no more, if it ever was at all.

Only a dark Eden remains.

OBSERVATIONS

Recorded some time later, after further consideration

Fears and Afflictions

I'll never know for sure why the seven were chosen or if the things we feared mattered. We probably could have been afraid of anything at all, so long as the fears were irrational. Whatever the answer, I think Rainsford had special knowledge of our situations. And although I can't prove it, I think he may have even caused some of our fears for his own purpose. In some cases he might have watched us for a long time, studying our personalities and our pasts with Dr. Stevens's help. But in other situations I think he instilled the fears in us from the start.

Do I believe Rainsford had something to do with Kate Hollander's car crash or Ben Dugan's discovery in the sandbox? Yes, I do. Connor's fear of heights, Alex and the dogs—it's easy enough to imagine how Rainsford might have manipulated those conditions over a period of years. I don't think he had anything to do with Keith's death or the death of Marisa's dad; but then again, I will never really know for sure. Whether or not he was involved, I have little doubt he was capable of setting these things in motion.

That leaves Avery, for whom there are many unanswered questions. I don't know why she feared death. I don't even know if she was ever cured. Was she killed during her treatment, then brought back to life? Maybe she had one of those fleeting moments at death's door, only to be pulled back from the brink at the last second. I believe she loves Davis; and oddly enough, I believe Davis loves her. I even think it might be part of the process—the power of love—which is at its most dangerous at fifteen or sixteen.

The Colors and
"The Masque of the Red Death"

Blue
Purple
Green
Orange
White
Violet
Black

For weeks and weeks I mulled over the colors of the rooms. Rainsford had a reason for everything, and I was convinced he had a reason for this, too. Putting them into a bunch of different search engines eventually gave me the answer.

Edgar Allan Poe had written a short story, like five pages long, called "The Masque of the Red Death." In it, a prince or a rich young ruler—it's hard to say which—closes himself off inside a castle with all of his privileged friends. Outside, a plague is ravaging the city, killing just about everyone; but inside, constant revelry permeates the castle. It's almost as if the prince in the story is daring the plague to try and find him. In the story there are seven rooms, each with its own brand of wicked fun. The seven rooms have the same colors as ours did, and in the story, the colored rooms appear in the same order.

At the end of "The Masque of the Red Death," the prince chases an uninvited masked guest. When the prince finally catches the intruder, the uninvited guest turns, and the prince falls dead on the spot. The guest in the story turns out to be death itself.

The message seems to be that no amount of money or privilege will stay the hand of death. But I believe Rainsford sees himself as not just privileged and rich, but as truly untouchable. Using the same colors as those in thc story is Rainsford's way of thumbing his nose at death. The setup is the same, but the result? Rainsford keeps winning. He keeps cheating death over and over again. I have to wonder though: does he worry? He must. He has to know that death can only be put off for so long. It will catch even him, and maybe that's why he chose the story of "The Masque of the Red Death," to remind himself that the end is coming whether he likes it or not.

The Pearl, The Woman in the Dunes, and Rainsford

I'm curious about when Rainsford first entered the world, but regardless of when it was, the use of *The Pearl* tells me a lot about his world view. It also makes me think Rainsford has been around for a long time, maybe as far back as the Dark Ages, when the caste system was still deeply embedded throughout the world.

In *The Pearl,* Kino goes underwater to find something that will change his life. My journey was like that, too. I went under*ground* to find something that would take away my fear. We all did. In Kino's case, what he found destroyed his family and his way of life. Though it seemed like a blessing, the pearl was a curse. For me and my friends, we discovered a place where fears are destroyed forever—but at what cost?

I think Rainsford believes in the idea that whatever station someone is born into is exactly where the person should remain. Kino found a pearl of great price and tried to use it in order to rise to a higher class. He only wanted a better life for his family and a slightly easier go of things. But soon enough Kino's life was in ruins.

I haven't spoken to Marisa about these things, but I think she's more like Kino than the rest of us. She tries to speak perfect English, and she doesn't want to talk about the past. I don't know, maybe for Marisa, language is like Kino's canoe, a symbol of leaving her heritage behind in pursuit of something that seems somehow better or safer.

The Woman in the Dunes, which I have now finished reading, has a slightly different take on things. In it a man is trying to find a rare insect, but what he's really looking for is a sort of immortality. If he can find the insect, he'll be remembered forever for having made the discovery (a paper-thin sort of immortality, but immortality just the same). His quest leads to ruin, and eventually he has to rethink what life and death mean. How strange that Rainsford has a similar problem: he is always here, and yet never remembered. What he does, he does in secret. No one knows who he is. He's like a ghost in that sense: ever-present, leaving no trace.

And lastly, his name, which I'm sure is a fairly new invention. He has had, I would imagine, many names. But Rainsford suits him pretty well in a totally ironic manner of speaking. In another story I discovered, "The Most Dangerous Game," there is a character named Rainsford. He's a big-game hunter, and he complains to his companion that he is always the hunter, never the hunted. He gets his wish when his boat lands on a strange island, where Rainsford becomes the game for a crazy hunter who is set on tracking him down and killing him. The funny thing? *I* was Rainsford at Fort Eden. We all were. The man doling out the cures was the hunter. This is one of the more curious things about the entire experience. Why did Rainsford use a name that makes him out to be the one being hunted? I think it goes back to the colors. I think Rainsford is being hunted by the most efficient killer of them all, and he knows it—a hunter who never, in the end, ever misses.

He's being hunted by death. And death has a 100 percent accuracy rating.

A Final Note

Rainsford could have done without all of these flourishes. He could have simply done the work and moved on, but he chooses to build his own bizarre narrative over time. It makes me wonder if he's not only a very bad man, but also an insane one, losing his mind in bits and pieces down through the ages.

I'm looking ahead now, sixty years to be exact, and I'm wondering what he will call himself when he returns to Fort Eden to repeat the trick. I wonder if Kino will still be floating down the floor to the elevator, or if someone else will be painted there. I wonder what Rainsford's name will be then.

Actually, there's only one thing I know for sure about that day. It's the thing I'm most certain about.

If I live another sixty years, I'll be waiting for him in the seventh room.

And if I have it my way, he won't get out alive.

DO YOU CRAVE ANOTHER CURE?

TAKE A SNEAK PEEK AT

PATRICK CARMAN'S

"Any of you ever been in the pump house?" Mrs. Goring asked, breaking her silence as we came to the dock.

No one raised a hand as Connor leaned down and splashed water on his face, but all eyes were on the rundown wooden structure that sat next to the pond. It was small, like the gardening shed in my backyard at home, and it looked like it might not make it through a hard winter.

"It's not really a pump house," Mrs. Goring continued. Then she walked away in the direction of the thing we were talking about and left us all scratching our heads about what was really inside.

"Why do we all have to go down there?" asked Ben. "Why not just Will? He got us into this mess."

"Did not," I said. Getting dumped on was growing old fast. "We all got cured, we all got symptoms. How is any of that my fault?"

"I think we should all go," Connor said. "Come on, it'll be cool." And that, more than anything, is probably what got us to do it. In the end it was like a dare no one wanted to miss out on. And there was the promise of a cure, even if the promise was made by an insane woman living all alone in the woods. It was something to hold on to.

"At least make him go first," Alex said. "That way if I fall I'll land on his head."

Marisa didn't come to my defense. She wouldn't even look at me. It got worse when Connor started whispering to her, glancing over his shoulder as I fumed.

She's back on the market. Nice. That's what his muscle-headed look told me, and Marisa didn't do anything to make him think otherwise.

"Fine, I'll go first," I yelled, blowing past everyone and arriving inside, where a metal door with a latch sat against the ground. Mrs. Goring knelt down beside me and grabbed the lever with her hand, shoving it sideways with a grinding noise that reverberated into places I couldn't see.

"He's older than seven hundred," Mrs. Goring whispered close to my ear, and I turned to her. "Let's make sure he doesn't see one more bloody year."

She shoved something in my hand and looked at me as if it was to remain our secret, whatever it was. Did I really think it was a good idea to conspire with Mrs. Goring again? She'd gotten me in a heap of trouble with Marisa and the rest, and yet I had a weird feeling I should let it pass. It crossed my mind to tell her about what I'd found in the woods, but there was no time.

"Agreed," I said, staring down a long, wide tube with a metal ladder on one side. There was faint, crackling light coming from somewhere far below. I slid what she'd handed me into my back pocket and listened carefully for any sound coming from the depths of whatever lay below ground at Fort Eden.

"Good thing you're not afraid of heights, Connor," I

said, imagining the old Connor Bloom, the one who had been terrified of falling.

I started down the ladder, feeling the rungs grow colder as I went, and immediately decided it was a bad idea. I stopped and started to complain, to reason with the others that we should go back, but Connor was the second one into the tube and he wouldn't stop coming toward me. His body was a hulking shadow against the light of the world outside.

"Go, man! I don't want to be down here all day."

I didn't move. I could feel the stupidness of what we were doing. It suddenly felt all wrong, just in time to have no power over what was happening to me.

"I'm going to step on your hand," said Connor. He was staring down at me from above with a resolve that bordered on psychotic. "I'm getting those vials, and you're going to help me do it. Move."

He placed one shoe on my left hand and began pressing down with his weight. Looking down, I saw that it was at least thirty feet more to the bottom.

"Okay, okay!" I shouted. "Back off!"

Connor removed his foot and I reluctantly went down another four rungs as someone else came in behind Connor, I couldn't tell who.

If I could just keep Marisa out of here. At least that would be something, I thought. But I kept on, Connor's relentless feet at my head, until I stood on a slick concrete floor and stared up. I could see all of them marching down the ladder in a line like little soldiers.

And at the very top, Mrs. Goring's head, which suddenly disappeared.

And that's when the metal door at the top of the ladder slammed shut, before half of us were even off the ladder.

I heard the handle turn way up there, grinding into the locked position, so it had to be loud. When everyone made it to the bottom, no one wanted to say what was really going on. We just stood there, still and quiet, and tried to come to grips with the reality of our circumstances.

We'd driven two hours out of L.A., walked down a very long and steep path into a desolate wood known by only a few. We'd trusted a crazy woman and let her lead us a hundred feet underground.

And we'd let her close the door on us.

We were trapped.